HENRY AND TOM

HENRY AND TOM

Michael Atkins and Wid Bastian

ISBN-13: 978-0692303276
ISBN-10: 0692303278

Praise for Henry and Tom

"Henry and Tom is beautifully written and filled with powerful and moving images…Tom's story is also grand and inspirational as the man rediscovers the dreams he had put on hold for far too long and sets out on his great adventure."

~**Readers Favorite** - (Starred Review)~

"Henry and Tom will make you think about who "we" (human animals) are who "they" (nonhuman animals) are, and is based on what we know about the meaningful friendships that form between different species…"

~**Dr. Marc Bekoff** - Professor Emeritus of Ecology and Evolutionary Biology University of Colorado, Boulder ~

"Spellbinding! Exquisitely penned with captivating imagery and a fascinating plot that inspires the heart and engages the mind. This gratifying work my Michael Atkins and Wid Bastion is crafted to leave the reader marveling at the wonders of the ocean and the power of dreams"

~**S.S.Segran** – Award-winning author of Aegis Rising~

"This is the book you've been waiting for…Amazing fiction that will take you to places you want to go…"

~**Ed Tyll** - Award Winning News Journalist~

Chapter One

Tom was up half an hour before sunrise. He did his best not to disturb Sydney; she preferred to sleep in until the last possible moment before going to work. He kissed his new wife softly on the cheek. She stirred, but did not wake up. Tom slid out of bed and into his running shorts and T-shirt.

Coffee was a must. Both Tom and Syd loved Kona coffee and although it was expensive, it was one of the few luxuries they both agreed was mandatory. Drinking his java, Tom watched out of his kitchen window as his neighbor Ron stood on his front porch monitoring his dog Fred while the pooch relieved himself on the front lawn. Tom missed owning a dog. His beloved Lacey, a black lab/Australian healer mix, had died a year earlier.

Lacey's passing might have been just as well – not only was she old at twelve, Sydney was allergic to dogs and cats and to any other furry creature with four legs. Tom was coming to terms with the reality that the rest of his adulthood would be lived sans pets. It was a tradeoff Tom Campbell was willing to make because he adored his new wife. Still, the idea of going through life without animal companions was difficult for Tom to accept. He had always had a pet, usually more than one. But not Syd

– not only did her allergies make that impossible, her parents simply would not tolerate the mess and hassle of owning a dog or cat or even a hamster.

Sydney Campbell was a very attractive woman. Her looks were deliberately understated and her husband liked it that way. Tom told her, and meant it, that she looked best naked. Syd wore makeup, but it was applied sparingly. She was tall, almost six feet, so she almost never wore heels because they made her feel self-conscious about her height. Her model like frame, thin with curves in all the right places, was usually obscured by trendy, but loose fitting, clothes. The only time Tom caught men admiring Syd was when they went to the beach and she was in her bikini.

Fourteen months ago Tom walked into a small café he frequented near Mission Beach. It was late in the afternoon. He had just finished a vigorous "old man" (Tom was almost thirty at the time) volleyball game on the beach and was sweaty and sandy. He was starving, so he popped in for a quick burger and fries. But from the second he walked in, he forgot about food.

Sydney Rogers was sitting with a girlfriend on the outdoor patio. She was wearing a pair of mid-length red shorts and a white top. She had on mirror shades and her jet black hair was wrapped in a tight bun. Tom was not normally the type of man to stare at women or to approach women he did not know in public places. While he was by no means conservative, Tom was not a "player" in any sense of the word. His last relationship had ended months ago in a less than amicable separation.

The first thing Tom did was look for a ring on her finger. Seeing none, he bought a Snapple and took a seat across from Sydney and pretended to read a local community paper as he sipped his drink. Because he was less than four feet away from them and it was not too noisy, Tom could hear the women's conversation.

"I'm still lost. Why is Dr. Jansen upset with you?" Sydney's friend asked.

"He did not like my approach. He said that my proposed dissertation 'lacked depth'. Evidently exploring the dynamic between siblings raised in an alcoholic home is not a sexy enough topic for him," Sydney answered.

"Sounds boring to me too," the friend teased.

"Thanks so much for your support, Jen. I'll remind you of this conversation the next time I'm sitting on your couch consoling you as you cry your eyes out over your latest loser boyfriend."

"Touché," Jen said.

"Any new prospects?" Syd asked.

"Nope, all dry on the man front. You?"

"Not looking. Too busy," Syd replied.

Jen leaned over close to Sydney and whispered, "You might want to look to your left."

Tom, being very much not slick, was staring at Sydney without his sunglasses on. He was not wise enough to know that her friend was giving Syd a heads up to his attentions. When Sydney suddenly looked to her left, Tom was nailed.

"Hi," Tom said. The word sounded lame, pathetic even, coming out of his mouth. Tom felt like he was a sixteen year old pimply faced kid again drooling over the head cheerleader in high school.

Sydney laughed – not at Tom, but at the situation. She was impressed that Tom simply said hello and didn't try and hide his interest in her.

"Come here often handsome?" Jen said, giggling.

"He was saying hello to me, Jen. How rude," Sydney teased.

"Yes, ah... hello. Hello to both of you," Tom stammered.

"You look like you've been playing on the beach," Jen said.

"Volleyball. Yea, I could use a shower, no doubt."

"Your place or mine," Jen teased. Jen Garrett was an insufferable flirt. When she saw that she was making Tom uncomfortable –

translation, he was a nice guy, not some pretentious jerk on the make – she turned up the heat.

Tom blushed. Sydney noticed that and liked it.

"Ignore my friend; she can be an idiot at times. I'm sorry; I didn't catch your name," Sydney said.

"Tom," Tom said, reaching out to shake Sydney's hand. "Tom Campbell."

"Sydney Rogers," Syd replied as she shook Tom's hand.

"*Doctor* Sydney Rogers," Jen added. "I'm Jen."

"Nice to meet you both. Doctor of what?" Tom asked.

"I'm a psychologist," Sydney replied. "Or I will be in a few months if I can get my dissertation approved."

"You're studying at UCSD?" Tom asked.

"I am, where do you -."

Sydney was interrupted by her friend. "Hey, I've seen you. You're on TV once in a while. You're that guy from Scripps, aren't you?"

"I'm the Director of Public Relations at Scripps, yes. I make statements to the press, meet with donors and handle all aspects of media relations," Tom explained.

"Are you an oceanographer?" Sydney asked.

"No, once upon a time I thought about becoming one or a marine biologist, but my talents lie elsewhere."

"I'll bet they do," Jen said, leaving no doubt that she was making a play for Tom.

"You're good a public speaking then? Speaking to small groups as well?" Sydney said as she shot a quick glare at Jen that clearly conveyed the message, "back off".

"I speak with people or groups on almost a daily basis," Tom confirmed.

"God, I need your help! Would you be willing to coach me a bit? I have to present my dissertation proposal next week and I'm scared to death," Sydney asked.

"Sure," Tom said, trying not to jump out of his shoes with enthusiasm. "I mean, of course. How do I -."

"Call me," Sydney said. "I'll work around your schedule. What luck! I was so worried." Sydney handed Tom her phone number written on a napkin.

"You guys need me to leave now? I mean if you two want to be alone I understand," Jen said.

"What if we name our first born daughter after you?" Tom joked.

Sydney liked that too. Tom caught on to the situation and teased Jen right back. When Tom stood to leave, it didn't hurt his prospects with Syd that he looked great in his shorts and tight shirt.

"You'll call me? For sure?" Sydney asked.

"Your phone is already ringing," Tom said as he tossed his Snapple bottle in the trash. "Nice to meet both of you."

"Why is it that the nice guys always go for you?" Jen said after Tom walked away.

"He did seem like a nice man, didn't he. I really do desperately need help with my public speaking, you know that," Syd said.

"What you desperately need to do is to get laid," Jen said.

"Yea, there's that too," Sydney agreed.

Six months later Tom and Sydney were married. Jen was Syd's maid of honor, but they refused to name their first daughter after her. Their first daughter would be named Jessica, after Sydney's beloved grandmother.

◊   ◊   ◊

Tom was packing his briefcase and setting out his suit when he felt Sydney come up from behind him and put her arms around him.

"I woke you up. Sorry honey," Tom said as he turned around and kissed his wife.

"That's okay. I was dreaming about you anyway," Sydney said.

"Nightmare?" Tom asked.

"Just the opposite," Syd replied.

Forty five minutes later Tom headed out for his run on the beach. He'd have to cut his morning jog short today in order to be at work on time, or at least be reasonably late. That was fine with him because being with Sydney was spectacular. There was nothing better in the world.

The "June gloom" fog, still around in July, was heavy as Tom began to run. Instead of winding his way through the neighborhood, Tom ran directly towards the beach.

Chapter Two

Earlier that morning while Tom and Sydney were still sleeping, two sperm whales, a cow and her calf, were swimming close to the surface five miles to the west of Pacific Beach. Out to sea there was no fog, so the night was warm and clear. The full moon was illuminating the calm water. They were not moving towards any specific destination. Their pod, three other cows and two more calves, traveled up and down the California and Mexican coasts year round.

Food was plentiful in the area. Large squid were found in abundance in deeper waters. Fish of many varieties, as well as octopus and skates, could be taken closer to shore. The cows had no enemies here and the calves were rapidly reaching the size where even the largest sharks and orcas were no threat to them.

The cow communicated with her calf and sister whales by clicking. The pod's coda (group of clicks) was unique both in terms of its language and its messages, which represented objects, information and actions pertinent to the whales. Their eyesight was very poor and used only for short distance object recognition. The whales used echolocation to scan and interpret their ocean environment.

The whales could hear the whishing sound of objects traveling on the surface of the water moving towards them. They were accustomed to encountering these objects and sounds. The whales knew that the small creatures that lived on land used these objects to carry themselves over the waves.

There was, in the collective memory of the pod, a notion that these land creatures that moved on top of the water could be dangerous, even a predator, but it had been a very long time since any whale in these waters was attacked by these creatures. In fact, the whales had recent memories and thoughts about these land animals being very curious about them. Especially when the sun was at its highest point in the sky, smaller floating objects with many land creatures in them could often be found sitting still on the surface as the whales swam by.

The mother cow clicked to her calf. They would not be joining the rest of the pod as they dove to feed. For now, they were content to swim along at a slow but steady pace. They would rejoin the rest of the pod after a period of time.

The U.S. Navy had three surface ships in the area on maneuvers, all cruisers. Their mission was to test the latest mid-frequency sonar. Active sonar, the method the Navy had used for decades to detect and track submarines, now had insufficient range. Especially when used at levels above 235 decibels, the new mid-frequency sonar was proving to be highly effective at finding and tracking nuclear submarines.

Somewhere in the general area a Navy attack sub was running silent and deep. When the exercises began, the cruisers' job was to use their new sonar to find and track the sub.

The sound made by a Saturn V rocket taking off is around 235 decibels. Sperm whales can also produce sounds of this magnitude and often do when communicating with other whales over long distances. Within and across pods, sperm whales have a system of ethics that they strictly adhere to regarding echolocation. Unless there is sufficient separation, a sperm whale will not blast another sperm whale with a deafening coda. If the whales did not practice these self-restrictions when broadcasting their clicks they could easily deafen or otherwise injure each other, especially their calves.

The water was relatively quiet as the cruisers approached the cow and calf. Off in the distance the cow could hear her sisters sounding as they dove, but their clicks were faint. The cow could tell that the objects that moved on the surface were getting closer to them, so she stopped and signaled her calf to stop as well. They were hovering twenty feet or so beneath the surface.

Without warning, a cruiser let loose a blast of sound in excess of 250 decibels. They were beginning their exercise. After a few seconds interval, a second cruiser released another deafening ping. The third cruiser followed up with a third sonar burst.

The cow had no warning that she was about to be hit by these sound waves. She was two hundred yards away from the first cruiser when the sonar blasted her. The calf, because he was swimming closely by her side away from the ships, was shielded a bit from the sound, but he was also stunned. The cow stopped moving and slowly floated to the surface. The lead cruiser was headed straight for her.

For whatever reason, perhaps due to the dim pre-dawn lighting, the first cruiser did not see or otherwise detect the whale's presence. The cow was regaining some of her senses and while she could not move quickly enough to avoid getting struck by the ship, she was able to shove her calf away at the last second. The cruiser's bow struck the cow mid-body, opening up a terrible gash. Then the propellers ripped another hole in her on the top of her head. The calf was still stunned from the sonar blasts, but the ship did not hit him.

The ships immediately stopped. The cow floated to the surface; she was deafened and severely injured. The calf sent out his codas to his mother, but she did not respond at first. Bright lights coming from the objects that were floating on the surface now lit up the ocean all around the whales. The calf could see blood flowing from his mother into the water – the sea all around him was turning red. Slowly, the calf was regaining his hearing.

Time passed as the objects on top of the water circled the whales. The cow gradually regained some of her senses and signaled to her calf. The calf responded by nudging his mother, encouraging her to swim. But the cow was mortally injured. While she could move to a small degree, she would never swim again.

When the light was about to rise in the sky, the objects on top of the water left the area. The cow was losing a great deal of blood and the blood trail now extended for half a mile. She sent out a repeating set of codas to her calf and nudged him away from her. The calf responded to these nudges by moving closer to his mother, not farther away.

After a period of time and extensive clicking by the cow, the calf eventually moved off to a position a hundred feet or so beneath her. He then let out a series of loud codas directed towards the depths and to the west of their position. He was signaling to the pod. He signaled once more, then again. He heard nothing in return.

When the calf swam back up to rejoin his mother, three great white sharks were circling the cow and posturing for attack. The first shark tore into the cow near her mid-body injury, removing a large chunk of flesh. Then the second bit the cow near the same wound. The third joined in the feeding frenzy.

The cow was sending out codas in rapid succession – the same message over and over. The calf was receiving the message, but he was not responding. The sharks continued to rip into the cow. All the calf could do was to watch the horror helplessly from below.

Suddenly two more great whites showed up. They bit the cow from the opposite side, as if to avoid conflict with the other three sharks. The mother whale let out a very loud series of sound blasts as if she was screaming at her calf, imploring him to do something.

As the calf hovered, he felt a sharp pain in his fluke. Reacting, he turned in the water and saw a great white right behind him. The shark had just taken a chunk out of his tail. Another great white joined the first and began to circle the calf.

The calf suddenly turned east and swam as fast he could. He was sending out codas as he swam. Two of the great whites pursued him. As the calf headed east, he could see the light penetrating the water just above him. His fluke was bleeding profusely, which kept the sharks engaged.

Because the calf had a head start, he was able to keep in front of the pursuing sharks. He could still hear his mother calling out, but her sounds were growing faint. Her message was the same, however. Her coda had not changed. The calf was moving at near top speed, twenty miles per hour, and the sharks were no more than thirty yards behind him.

The sea was rapidly getting shallow. The calf knew that the water eventually ended and land began. To get so close to shore was dangerous, but the sharks were still in hot pursuit.

The calf was in a panic, completely traumatized by watching his mother get struck by a ship and attacked by the sharks. He did not slow down until he could swim no more because now he was stranded on the beach.

Chapter Three

Tom felt at peace. Everything was right with the world when he was jogging. Today especially; after enjoying an early morning romp with his wife Tom was in a terrific mood.

Unfortunately, his *Walkman* was not cooperating. He quickly realized that it had quit on him because he forgot to change the batteries. Oh well, no more *U2* singing in his ears. He would make the rest of his run with the world as background noise. He continued to jog south on the beach, sticking close to the surf line where the sand was firm.

The fog was heavy. While it normally cleared before noon, at seven thirty visibility was limited to less than thirty feet. Tom heard something before he saw anything. It sounded to him like something huge crashed onto the shore out of the surf. He heard a couple of loud, dull thumps.

Then he saw the whale. The sight of a juvenile sperm whale, eighteen feet long and weighing in excess of a ton, floundering on the beach stopped him dead in his tracks. Evidently the whale had just beached himself because he was still glistening with water and flopping around vigorously.

"My God!" Tom exclaimed. The whale was magnificent to behold. Tom had seen both adult and juvenile sperm whales before on the open sea, but to look at one up close and personal on the beach was awe inspiring.

The calf was slapping his tail against the sand. The first thought Tom had was, why in the world was this whale here?

Sperm whales did not normally beach themselves, unlike some other whale species. Searching his memory, Tom could not recall a sperm whale beaching himself in San Diego County for at least the past twenty years.

When he approached the young whale, he saw that his fluke had been bitten. Must have been a shark or an orca that attacked him, Tom assumed. While Tom was not an expert on whales, he knew quite a lot about them. Sharks and orcas were the only predators big enough to attack a whale of this size.

Tom wondered how close he could, or should, get to the whale. As he approached the calf, the whale opened its eye and looked straight at him.

"Hey there," Tom said, not knowing how to address a sperm whale properly. "Looks like you've had a rough morning."

The calf stopped floundering when he saw Tom. He started to click. Tom heard him.

"Sorry," Tom said. "I don't speak sperm whale. But I know some people who do."

Tom took his cell phone from his pocket, flipped it open and dialed Scripps. He asked for George Walker, the head of the Cetacean Department.

"Tom, good morning. I know that I haven't gotten you that information you requested on -."

"George, that's not why I'm calling."

"Okay then, what can I do for you?"

"I'm looking at a juvenile sperm whale. He's about twenty feet long. He needs your help."

"Out for an early morning sail, are you? The whale just came up to your boat and said hello?"

"I'm standing on Pacific Beach, about a quarter mile south of where Balboa Avenue meets the water. The whale is on the beach with me."

"What?" George said, not believing his ears.

"From the looks of him I think he beached himself less than five minutes ago. I heard him hit the sand."

"Holy crap. I… okay. We're on it. Stay with the whale, Tom. It might be an hour before we can get there in force. Is there anyone else with you?"

"Not yet, but this whale is going to attract attention."

"Is the whale visibly injured?"

"It looks like a shark or an orca took a chunk out of his fluke, but I don't think it's enough to kill him."

"Wait a minute… What's this? Stand by." George put Tom on hold.

"Help is on the way, my friend. These people know all there is to know about whales," Tom reassured the calf.

A minute later George popped back on the line. "The Navy reports that one of their cruisers collided with and severely injured a cow sperm whale early this morning a few miles from your position. She had a calf. You have to be with her calf, Tom."

"The cow is dead?"

"The Navy assumes so. They were on maneuvers testing their latest sonar and the whale was in the wrong place at the wrong time. Tragic."

"That explains it then."

"What?" George asked.

"I'm looking at fins in the water. A couple of great whites are cruising just off shore. No doubt I'm standing next to their intended meal."

"Stay there. Keep the lookie loos away from the whale and for God's sakes don't let people touch him or disturb him in any way. Understood?"

"I'm on duty as whale body guard. Understood."

"We're on our way," George said and then hung up.

When George hung up, the first of the curious arrived. They were a couple of surfers from the looks of them, both kids in high school or just out of high school.

"Totally rad," the scruffier of the two boys said.

"Yea, gotta get a picture of this," the other kid said.

"Keep your distance boys," Tom ordered. "Scripps is on the way. They're going to help him get back in the water."

"Who are you? A cop? This your whale or somethin'?" the shaggy teenager challenged. Clearly the boys were intent on getting close to the whale despite Tom's warning.

Then one of the boys reached out his hand to touch the whale's back. Tom pulled the boy's arm away and in a sure, swift move took his legs out from under him and tossed him on the sand.

"Don't touch the whale," Tom said, as calmly as possible.

"That's assault man!" the boy shouted.

"If you try and touch the whale I'll knock your ass to the ground again and this time not so gently. Stand back, please."

Sirens in the distance tempered the boys' desire for a confrontation. They could see the flashing lights headed up the beach. The kids backed off and started snapping pictures.

Tom sat by the whale on the beach side as more people approached. The whale was calmer now, or at least outwardly appeared to be so.

"Must have been a nightmare for you," Tom said. He realized that he was talking to the whale as if he was a person, which made little sense, but for some reason Tom thought it might help the calf to cope.

The calf clicked after Tom spoke to him. Maybe I am getting through on some level, Tom rationalized.

"I lost my mom when I was a kid too," Tom said. "There is nothing worse than losing your mom."

The whale clicked again. The San Diego County Sheriffs then arrived and hopped out of their truck.

"Are you Tom Campbell?" the deputy sheriff asked.

"Yes, sir," Tom replied.

"You work at Scripps, right?"

"Yes, sir," Tom replied again.

"Good. You're in charge then until the rescue team arrives. We'll secure the area. Anything else we can do?" the deputy asked.

"Keep people out of the water. See those fins out there?" Tom said, pointing at the large dorsal fins cruising along just past the surf line. "Those fellas have been denied a meal. Probably best not to offer them a substitute."

Chapter Four

By ten a.m. the beach was packed with a couple of hundred curious bystanders, camera crews and reporters from the local and national media. The Sheriffs were doing their job – the only person allowed near the whale was Tom. Everyone else was corralled at least twenty yards away behind a police line.

George Walker had relayed the basic rescue plan to Tom on the phone. High tide was going to be near sunset – that was the best time to try and get the whale back in the water. The resources to accomplish this amazing feat would be arriving shortly. Three loaders would be used to roll the whale gently over on to two enormous rubber straps that were eight feet wide and twenty feet long. The straps were being supplied by nearby Sea World where they were used to lift Orcas and move them from pool to pool. Once the straps were beneath the whale, two carry deck cranes with the capacity to lift over 10,000 pounds each would lift the whale off of the sand and move him in the straps out into the surf. Temporary metal tracks would allow the cranes to move into almost eight feet of water without being swamped. At that point the straps would be disconnected from the crane and, in theory, the whale could then swim back into the open ocean.

Sea World vets were also en route. From Tom's description of the wound on the whale's fluke, they thought they could treat it with antibiotics and a special gel like application that seals the wound for a time even in salt water.

Tom continued to talk with the whale. He wasn't sure if he was doing any good at all, but from what the Sea World and Scripps people were telling him if the whale kept gently stirring and opening and closing his eyes he was doing as well as possible under the circumstances.

"... so that's how they are going to do it. They know that they have to push and lift you very gently. Outside of the water all of your weight is killing you by pressing down on your lungs and heart. We have to get you back out to sea in the next few hours."

Tom looked into the whale's eye as much as possible. He avoided touching the whale because George told him that it could be harmful. They did catch a weather break – the fog was not lifting. That kept the summer sun from beating down on the calf. The temperature was a moderate 69 degrees.

"What's it like to be a whale, I wonder?" Tom said, filling time. "You're an intelligent creature, we know that. What do you think about?"

The whale was still clicking every so often – more so when Tom spoke to him. This was another very good sign according to the experts. Tom's voice seemed to calm the whale down, which was very important to his survival out of the water.

Just then, the crowd was parted by the police as the Scripps people and the equipment arrived. George was in the lead car, the loaders and the deck cranes were right behind him on semi-truck trailers. Behind the semis, a twenty foot cube truck with the *Sea World* logo on its side rounded out the convoy.

"Tom! I've been watching this on TV, but to see the whale up close is unbelievable. He is in pretty good shape," George said as he stepped from his truck onto the sand.

"We've been talking all morning, sharing stories. I wish I understood what his clicks meant," Tom said. "Is the plan still a go?"

"Absolutely. It's not like we do this every day, or any day for that matter. But we've checked with all the experts we could find and this method seems like our best shot at success."

"Did you bring -."

"Your clothes are in the back of the truck; a pair of jeans and a Scripps shirt. You can clean up too. We brought soap and water and food if you're hungry."

"Give me a few, will ya? I'm going to do a quick change, call Syd and then ring my boss. I expect I have to talk with the media. Even though I'm part of this story, I'm still the media rep," Tom said.

As Tom walked to the truck and opened the door, he heard the whale thrashing about and flapping his tail on the sand as if he was in distress. The vets were just starting to attend to him. People from Scripps and Sea World were gathered all around the whale. They stepped back because the calf wasn't calm any longer.

Tom quickly turned and walked back over to the whale. When the whale saw Tom, he stopped flopping around. The whale seemed to have imprinted on Tom's voice and presence.

"Okay, maybe we better hold up some towels for cover right here so you can change clothes on the beach. The calf does not like it when you're out of his sight and can't hear you," George said.

"Come on," Tom said. "Really? How can that be?"

"Let's experiment," George said. Then he yelled, "Everybody back off." Speaking at normal volume, George asked Tom, "Walk away again and let's see what happens."

As Tom walked out of the whale's field of vision, the calf started to thrash about. He quickly returned to where the calf could see him and started talking to him, reassuring him.

"I think you better stay close," George said. "If the calf does much more of that we may not be able to save him."

So Tom Campbell changed clothes, talked on his cell phone and ate a quick lunch next to his new best friend, a three thousand pound cetacean. The vets worked on the calf's fluke. The whale didn't put up much of a fuss as they dressed the wound as best they could. They also buried protection posts in the sand on either side of the tail just to be on the safe side in case the whale thrashed too much. Getting whipped by the tail of a juvenile sperm whale could seriously injure someone.

Tom was also now in charge of keeping the whale wet. A fire truck parked nearby was pumping fresh seawater into a hose Tom used to soak the whale every few minutes or so.

Reluctantly, the Sheriff was forced by orders sent down through the chain of command to allow limited media access to the whale. The media were now permitted to get close to the calf for a few minutes, one reporter and one camera person at a time.

"You're Tom Campbell, right?" the female reporter asked. She looked to Tom to be no more than twenty five.

"I'm Tom Campbell," Tom replied. He was busy talking to the whale, distracting the creature as crews were laying down the metal tracks for the cranes to use to carry him back into the ocean.

"Can I ask you a few questions? The camera is off now."

Tom did not want to answer questions at the moment, but he was the PR person at Scripps. Appearing rude or uncooperative with the media, especially with the local TV stations, was not in his best interest.

"Sure, go ahead," Tom said. He put down the hose.

After hurrying through a brief intro for her news story the reporter asked, "You found the whale?"

"I was the first person to see him on the beach, yes," Tom answered.

"You're the Head of Public Relations for Scripps, right Mr. Campbell?"

"I am, yes."

"Why are you attending to the whale? Aren't there marine biologists who might be more qualified than you to see to the calf?"

"The whale seems to get agitated when I leave his line of sight and when he can't hear me. George Walker, the marine biologist from Scripps who is charge here, asked me to stay with him."

"You've made friends with a whale! That's extraordinary. Have you given the whale a name?"

"A name? Like a person's name?"

"Yes."

"No, he's a whale. I'm just trying to keep him calm."

The Sheriff gave the reporter the high sign, telling her to wrap it up. She shut off her camera and walked a few yards away from the calf. Then she recorded the end of her piece using the stranded whale as background, "Tom Campbell, Chief Spokesperson for Scripps, has found himself in the unlikely position of whale sitter as the crews are working…"

Sydney laughed as she switched off the TV set at home. Her husband was a whale-talker!

If Tom has those kinds of skills, maybe I should re-think my no pets rule, Syd laughed to herself. She took out her keys, locked up the house and hopped in her Toyota. It was time for her to go and investigate this whale business in person.

Chapter Five

The calf was not sure what the land creatures were doing. The land animal he knew best, the one who was there from the time he escaped from the sharks by swimming on to the sand, was still right next to him. As long as this land creature stayed by his side the calf felt somewhat safe.

Breathing was becoming harder to do. The calf knew that being out of the water, away from home, was not good for him. But when the calf thought about swimming his mind was flooded with thoughts of his mother being eaten alive before his eyes and the sharks chasing him and trying to devour him. He desperately wanted to swim, but he was also very afraid to go back into the ocean.

The land creature he trusted was making sounds again. The calf clicked back the simple message that he wanted the land creature to stay close to him. As the land creature kept making sounds, the calf heard other objects – these were not small land creatures, but rather something else - making a loud noise. They reminded the whale of the objects the land creatures used to float on the surface of the ocean, only these objects moved on the sand.

The whale was frightened by these loud noises and even more scared when the objects moved towards him and touched his body. He reacted by flopping around and slapping his tail on the sand. The objects moved away from the whale, but they kept making noise.

Then the land creature the whale trusted looked directly into the whale's eye. He was making sounds again. The whale clicked back the message, "I am scared". The land creature then did something he had not done before; he touched the whale and stroked his body. The calf felt slightly calmer when the land creature touched him. He stopped floundering on the sand. The more the whale resisted and moved, the harder it was to breathe.

Click, click, click. The whale sent out the coda message, "I'm scared, please help me; I'm scared, please help me" over and over the whale clicked, hoping that the land creature could understand him.

Looking directly into the land creature's eyes, at least what the whale thought were his eyes, they were so small, the calf sensed something. He sensed that this land creature, and the other creatures and objects nearby, were only trying to help him. They meant him no harm. He had to allow them to do what they were going to do, or he was going to die.

Now the clicks changed. The coda sent this time was, "I agree, I agree, I agree." The objects then moved close to the whale and again touched his body. The calf did not react. The objects were pushing him, rolling him over. Frightened, but resigned to his fate, the calf did not resist. The sensation of rolling over on land was very different than it was at sea. In the ocean, the calf loved to roll and spin. On the sand, the sensation of rolling over was painful. For a moment, the whale was suffocating. Then, when he was righted again (on his belly) the whale could take in air once more. The calf was getting weak, very weak. His energy reserves were close to zero.

Underneath him the whale could now feel something other than sand. Whatever was beneath him now felt more like another whale; only it was colder, oddly shaped and it covered only a portion of his body. Now the whale could hear more objects making noise. These were new objects – larger and louder than the three objects that pushed him and rolled him.

The land creature the calf trusted was right by his eye. He had not left his side. The whale clicked again, "I'm scared, please help me; I'm scared, please help me". The land creature again stroked the whale and spoke to him. The calf felt a slight sensation of relief. As long as this land creature stayed near him the calf somehow felt that he could endure whatever it was that was going to happen to him.

Making even louder noises the new larger objects came close to him, but they did not touch the calf. A large number of the land creatures now moved all around the calf. After a short amount of time passed, the whale felt whatever was beneath him wrapping close around his body.

It was almost impossible to breathe now. The calf could see the sun for the first time since he had been on the sand. The sun was dipping into the ocean. The calf knew that this meant soon the light would be gone and the world would be dark for a time.

The land creature the calf trusted was once more right by his eye and he was making sounds. The calf clicked back, "I'm scared, please help me; I'm scared, please help me". After the land creature touched him again, the whale felt the very strange sensation of being lifted up in the air.

The objects on the sand right behind the calf were making even more noise. The calf could clearly see them out of his right eye. Now raised five feet in the air, the calf focused on the land creature he trusted who remained very close to him.

"I'm terrified, I'm terrified, I'm terrified," the calf clicked over and over.

Now the calf could feel the waves splashing up against his body. They were taking him back into the water! The objects making the loud noises were moving with him into the surf. The calf tried his best to keep taking breaths, but it soon became too hard. The land creature the calf trusted was right by his eye and touching him.

Now the clicks changed to "Please hurry, please hurry, please hurry."

When the object dropped the calf into the water, the whale felt the sensation of floating, even though his belly was still touching the sand. With the weight lifted off of his lungs, the calf was able to take in a deep breath. The water was soothing on his skin. For a moment the whale did not move – he just lay there in eight feet of water and rested – slowly breathing, coming back to life.

Now there were more land creatures all around him, but they were diving and swimming, not walking on the sand. There were also objects floating on the water. Then the calf remembered the sharks. Where were they? The calf slapped his tail against the water and clicked and then turned around, facing out to sea. He sensed no sharks near him. He swam out a few yards into the ocean. He was fully floating now and breathing normally.

Then he heard them. The pod was calling to him! His family was nearby! The calf clicked back loudly sending out the message, "I am here, I am here". The cows responded. The calf knew what to do – he had to swim to them. Once reunited with the pod the cows would protect and feed him and he would be safe.

The calf turned on his side and looked at one of the objects floating on the water. He saw what he was looking for, the land creature he trusted. He was floating on the object and looking down at the calf.

The calf clicked again, "I am safe, I am safe." But these clicks were not another message sent to the pod, they were a message sent to the land creature he trusted.

Although he did not know what the sound meant, the calf heard the land creature say loudly, "Goodbye Henry" as the whale swam away.

Chapter Six

"Holy crap!" Tom exclaimed as he got into Syd's Corolla and closed the door. The reporters were still not satisfied; they were banging on the car window demanding to be told more.

"Drive baby!" Tom yelled to his wife. Sydney put the car in gear and rolled away, slowly at first so she didn't flatten a reporter or a camera man. After a minute or so they were clear and they pulled out onto Mission Boulevard. It was almost nine p.m.

Sydney was laughing. "What's so damn funny?" Tom asked.

"You are honey. You'd think you were President Clinton or something. Those people would not leave you alone."

"Tell me about it. Tomorrow might not be any easier," Tom said.

"I do get it. It was a fantastic thing, but it was just a whale," Sydney reasoned. "There were media on the beach from all over the world. I had no idea that a stranded whale was international news."

"Sperm whales are magnificent creatures. You had to have read *Moby Dick* as a kid," Tom said as he continued to scroll through his voice mail messages, all fifty five of them.

"Nope, never did. Saw the old movie though. Loved Gregory Peck," Sydney said. "Hey, you've got to be starving. Want me to stop and get you something?"

"Nada. Let's go straight home, please. No more calls either – the cell, the home phone, the pagers, they all get turned off. I'm exhausted."

"I am so proud of you, Thomas. You hung in there like a trooper. I would have run away and hidden somewhere if all those reporters were after me," Sydney admitted. Since they were stopped at a light, she leaned over and gave Tom a kiss.

"It's really hard to express how cool it was to spend time with a whale," Tom said as he snapped his cell phone shut.

"I'll bet he smelled terrible. How could you stand it?" Sydney asked.

"He didn't smell bad. Well, not that bad anyway. I think we connected on some level. You should have seen it Syd; the whale would not let me out of his sight. I talked to the whale from early morning until he swam away at sunset."

"You talked to the whale, huh. Did he talk back?"

"He did actually. He clicked at me almost non-stop."

"Well, do share! What did he say?" Sydney teased.

"I'm serious. We made a real connection. I got that he was scared. Who wouldn't be? Those sharks tore his mother apart and took a bite out of his tail," Tom said, a bit agitated.

"He's a whale, Tom. You make him sound like a person. Whales aren't people."

"Maybe whales are smarter than people," Tom said, seriously but glibly.

"You're excited; that's all. Who wouldn't be! My husband is a celebrity!"

"Yea, thank God that won't last very long. I'll be old news within a week. Thanks for coming to get me."

"Wouldn't have missed it for the world, sweetheart," Sydney said. "Home sweet home."

The Campbells climbed out of their sedan and went inside. Their two bedroom duplex wasn't much, but they were saving every nickel for a down payment on a larger home. Tom had just gotten a raise at Scripps and Sydney was now an associate professor with a promising idea for a series of academic and popular books on addiction.

Their future was bright. They both wanted children, but they also wanted to wait a while. Syd was only twenty six; they had plenty of time to start a family.

Tom showered and put on a pair of shorts. Sydney was already asleep when he crawled in bed beside her. But he couldn't sleep. His mind was spinning thinking about the whale, the rescue, all of it.

He understood what Syd was trying to say – what happened to him was a highly emotional experience. It was all too easy to ascribe human-like characteristics to the whale under such circumstances. She was certainly not speaking anything but conventional wisdom. While Tom was not an expert on animal behavior, he knew that most scientists cringed anytime an observer talked about animals having emotions or complex and abstract thoughts.

Still, Tom knew, both rationally and intuitively, that he and the whale connected on a deep level. What they shared was beyond extraordinary. When he looked at the whale he swore that he saw something behind that big beautiful eye – not just intelligence, but something greater. For sure Tom sensed something far more than simply an animal as humans define animals.

Reaching over, Tom touched Syd's hair and gently played with it for a minute. She is so beautiful, Tom said to himself. I'm so lucky. Sydney is bright too – not just bright, near genius. What was this woman doing with the likes of me? Tom asked himself. He slid next to her and cuddled with her. Syd rolled on her side and they spooned.

As he closed his eyes and tried to go to sleep, Tom hoped that the calf had reunited with his pod. George told him that if the calf could rejoin his pod the chances of him surviving were high. He thought about Lacey too, how she would look at him and seem to know his thoughts, how she could anticipate his next moves with uncanny accuracy. He had no doubt that Lacey experienced emotions, all dogs do. To deny that was silly and stupid, Tom thought.

But animals are not people. Their inner world is unknown to us. What the whale thought and felt only the whale knows. Tom felt privileged to share in the whale's world as much as that was possible. Their day together would always remain one of the best days of his life, certainly the most unique day.

When Tom looked into the whale's eye, he thought about Henry. He didn't consciously choose to do so, it just happened - there was no doubt in his mind that the whale's name was Henry.

Where was Henry right now? Tom imagined the calf reunited with his pod, being fed and cared for and protected by them. He didn't want to believe that Henry was killed before he could reach safety. Henry's story absolutely needed to have a happy ending and Tom could not imagine it any other way.

Chapter Seven

June 2015
San Francisco, California

I hate this place, Tom thought as he walked into the legal offices of Garrett and Ham, Sydney's lawyers. He was thankful that this was likely the last time he would be forced to put on a smile and act pleasant when inside he was seething.

Everyone went out of their way to be polite here, to the point of being nauseating. But the alternative was worse and Tom knew it. An amicable separation and divorce had saved him and Sydney tens of thousands of dollars in legal fees and spared their kids the rancor that usually comes with a split after twenty years of marriage.

Waiting in the reception area, Tom was also happy that he did not have to sit through another mediation session with his lawyer, Sydney and her counselor. The only winners in that process were the attorneys. Tom imagined them getting together for cocktails after the day ended and joking about how much money they made dividing up other people's property.

Tom argued that mediation was unnecessary that he and Syd were quite capable of working everything out without outside intervention. Sydney did not disagree that they were capable of doing so, but she was afraid that they were too emotionally tied to the subject matter. She wanted to be equitable to Tom without getting shortchanged. The neutrality of bringing in a third party to settle a non-existent dispute made sense to her.

Tom wasn't sure just what made sense anymore.

"Hello Syd," Tom said. He walked over to her and they exchanged platonic cheek kisses.

"Hi Tom. Thanks for being flexible. I had to re-arrange my schedule around the event in Portland. You can still watch the kids next week, right?" Sydney asked.

"Yes, no problem," Tom answered.

"Thanks. As I told Sally, you and I close friends. Nothing will change that. Ever," Sydney said with pride.

Every time Sydney called him a "friend" Tom cringed inside. While he did not want to be her enemy, he damn sure did not want to be her friend. But Tom kept his mouth shut. It was time to get this over with; he had other things to attend to today.

"Syd, not to be too insistent but -."

"Yes; absolutely, Tom. I know you have to be somewhere else today. We still have time for lunch though, right?"

"Of course. A short one though Syd."

"Then let's get this over with so we can go and talk. Sally, are the papers all ready to sign?"

The lawyers then led Tom and Sydney Campbell through the twenty page divorce decree. Sydney kept the house, but she was required to sell it or re-finance it and give half the equity to Tom within two years. Their liquid and other physical assets were split roughly 50-50. They shared jointly legal custody of the children. Sydney waived her right to formal child support because she and Tom agreed on how the kids should be supported by both of them.

Ten minutes later and the review was finished. When the judge rubber stamped the documents later that month, Thomas and Sydney Campbell would no longer be husband and wife.

Tom and Syd chose to go to the main floor of the office building and sit in the café. It was normally not too crowded and the sandwiches were decent. Sydney respected Tom's need to run to an appointment – she did not want to delay him unduly.

"The usual?" Tom asked. Sydney almost always ordered the same meal – a turkey sandwich on rye, mustard only, with a vanilla yogurt and bottled water. Tom ordered his favorite – hot pastrami and potato salad with a light beer.

"Please," Syd said. "And let me pay this time. You don't have to always buy me lunch; I can return the favor on occasion." Sydney handed Tom a twenty and a ten dollar bill.

They sat down and started to eat. For a minute or so neither of them said a word.

"How are you feeling?" Sydney asked.

"Too 'therapist', Syd."

"Sorry, I'm not doing too well, Tom. Divorce sucks, even when it's done between people who like and respect each other. I'm sure this all very hard for you. I know it is for me."

"Empathy, okay. That's better, I guess."

"Tom, I'm sorry. Maybe this isn't a good time. Should I take my sandwich and go? I respect -."

"Sydney for God's sake! Just say what you need to say. Every statement does not have to be qualified or pre-positioned for maximum politeness."

"Are you still planning on going to Hawaii?" Sydney asked.

"Yes. I'm leaving in thirty days. My plans have not changed."

"I've thought a lot about this and consulted some experts. Now, I agree that you are an accomplished sailor. No doubt about that. But you are asking me to send my son out on a sailboat with you to cross half the Pacific Ocean. I cannot agree to that, Tom. I know that disappoints you and I'm sorry, but my decision is final."

"Have you told Jonas yet?" Tom knew that Syd would say no, after her well thought out and perfectly reasonable thought process had been thoroughly explained, of course.

"No. I thought the news might be best coming from you."

Tom laughed. He couldn't help himself; the laugh burst out without warning. Syd looked at him as if he had just insulted her mother.

"Sorry, Syd. No way. Your decision, your announcement. I will not be the fall guy on this one."

"He already blames me for the divorce and resents the hell out of me. If you would please -."

"Is he wrong for feeling that way? You're big on making 'I' statements. Taking responsibility, looking in the mirror, all that. Why shouldn't Jonas have some resentment towards you?"

"We've been over this. I thought we were past assigning blame. This is about Jonas, not us. You're better than that, Tom."

"Wow, okay. Syd, you're a good person. You love our kids, I know that. God knows I shoulder a great deal of blame for us drifting apart. But sometimes I think you believe your own bullshit just a little too much."

"My 'bullshit'?"

"This notion you have that human beings can think every problem through like little rational robots. People don't work that way, Syd."

"Is that so," Sydney was pouting, a mood Tom knew all too well.

"Syd, this hurts. I mean really hurts. Yes, I've known we were over for a year now, but actually signing the documents and finalizing everything... it's painful."

Sydney looked at Tom. Her pouting was over. She could see that he was in pain. She reached over and touched his hand. Tom squeezed her hand affectionately. They both teared up.

"Tom, what was I supposed to do? We are both such different people. You know that I never stopped loving you; it's just that... What we had as a couple, it's gone. I've never said that it was all your fault. I'm to blame too. We've talked about this so many -."

"Yes, I'm being ridiculous. Forgive me. I'm a grown man."

"Stop it. Now who's dispensing bullshit. You're a great person, Tom. You need to be with someone who is more like you – open, free, emotional, vibrant. Women are very interested in you. Maybe you should think about dating."

"I'm not interested in dating. I am interested in sailing."

"There's something else we need to discuss," Sydney said.

"Okay."

"I'm seeing someone, Tom. It's getting serious. You know him, Harold Frandsen."

"Your publisher?"

"Harold and I became friends. A few months ago our relationship developed into something more."

"You're going to marry him?"

"We haven't made that decision. But we are considering living together."

"Wow, that's great news. I'm so happy for you."

"Sarcasm. That's your response? Would you rather that I lied to you or just announced one day that Harold lives with me?"

"No, Syd. As usual you handled things in the most appropriate way. I've got to go, really I do."

"About Hawaii…"

"What about Hawaii?" Tom said as he stood.

"Are you really considering taking a job there?"

"Yes, I'd like to get back into a position with a marine institution. You know that I've not been happy with my career since I left Scripps."

"Jonas wants to move to Hawaii with you."

"I know."

"I won't allow that, Tom."

"You don't have a choice. Now that Jonas is fifteen, he chooses where he wants to live. That's the law in California."

"And if I object?"

"Then I guess you object, Syd. Jonas wants to live with me. He does not hate you, he loves you. Why not try and see this from his perspective?"

Tom was ready to walk away, but he did not want just to cut off Sydney. He knew that she would not do that to him.

"The sailing trip is out, Tom. I won't bend on that. The thought of Jonas, or you for that matter, out there all alone on the ocean scares me to death."

"I get that, Syd. I will respect your wishes regarding the trip. Jonas cannot go with me, but you have to tell him that, not me."

"Fair enough," Syd replied.

"Call me in a few days. I hope your book signing goes well. Harold lives in Portland, right?"

"Yes he does," Syd said sheepishly.

"Then I'm sure you'll be well looked after." Tom and Syd exchanged parting cheek kisses and Tom walked off. He was already late for his next appointment. It was an important meeting.

He was tendering his resignation. It was time to move on.

Chapter Eight

"Just like that?" Luke Hansen said. Luke was the Vice President of Pioneer Associated Insurance, the largest health insurance firm in Northern California.

"I'm giving you thirty days, Luke. Isn't that the standard protocol?" Tom said. He was fingering the cup of coffee Luke's secretary had given him, but he had yet to sample it.

"Let's discuss this. I know that the divorce has taken its toll on you. God knows we all want to start over from time to time and -."

"This is not about my very real mid-life crisis or about turning fifty, or about Sydney and I splitting up. I am done being the spokesman for a health care company. Don't get me wrong, Pioneer is a great corporation. I'm proud to have worked here for a decade, but I'm done and that's the plain and simple truth."

"You have a new job I suppose," Luke asked as he fidgeted with his pencil, incessantly tapping the eraser end on his desk.

"No, but I have a great prospect."

"Where may I ask?"

"The Hawaii Institute of Marine Biology. Their longtime head of fundraising and media relations is retiring. I have a shot at the job, but of course it's a highly sought after position."

"How much of a pay cut are we talking about?"

"Well, this year you upped my salary to $400,000. The Hawaii position pays $175,000, tops."

"What's your backup plan?" Luke asked.

"I don't have a backup plan. I'm going to sail to Hawaii and stay there. If I don't get the job at the Institute I will work on a dive boat or sell T shirts or something."

"Seriously?" Luke asked.

"Yes seriously. Syd made a ton of money over the past five years. We saved most of it and now I get half. I really don't need to work at all, especially after the house gets sold. Living in the hills and driving a Benz are things in my past. My future is much simpler and far less expensive."

"You'll be missed around here. You're the best at what you do, Tom. Everyone thinks dealing with the media is an easy job until they try it; then they quickly learn how hard it is."

"Thanks, Luke. You've been a great boss. Promise that you'll visit me in Hawaii. I'll teach you how to scuba."

"Go underwater with all the fishes and the sharks? No thanks. I'm lucky to work up the courage to swim in the deep end of the pool."

"Do I need to sign anything else?" Tom asked.

"No, we're done with the paperwork. Still planning on crossing the Pacific solo?"

"Just half of it," Tom said.

"You're completely insane; you know that, don't you?"

◊   ◊   ◊

"That's insane Dad, and so unfair. What if I say I'm going anyway? Are you going to kick me off the boat?" Jonas Campbell was angry. When he came home from school today, his mother told him that she was not allowing him to sail with his father to Hawaii.

"Actually, your mother has a point. Sailing that far is dangerous. I think the risk is justified given the rewards, but your mother loves you and worries about you."

"She just doesn't want me to live with you. That would make her look bad to all of her other shrink buddies."

"That's not true, Jonas. As far living with me goes, once I'm set up you're with me if that's what you want."

"Really?"

"Really," Tom said.

"What if mom says no?"

"She does not have the final say on that one – you and I do."

"I want to sail with you. Can't you just tell mom that I'm going and that's that? Put your foot down."

"It's not like that, Jonas. She has a right to object to something as adventurous as sailing to Hawaii. You know that your mother is scared to death of the water."

"She goes sailing with Harold," Jessica Campbell said. So far Jess had stayed on the sidelines of the conversation, preferring to play with her *i Pad* and listen to music on her headphones.

"I doubt that," Tom said. "Your mother is allergic to sailboats."

"She doesn't seem to be allergic to Harold's boat. I think she likes it better than yours because it's so much bigger." Jess handed her father her *i Pad*. On the screen was a photo of Sydney wrapped in Harold's arms standing on the deck of what had to be a forty foot sailboat. Tom recognized the Oregon coast in the background.

"She has no problem coming on board for a meal or to spend the day. But your mother becomes terrified as soon as the boat leaves the harbor," Tom added.

Jessica took her phone back from her dad and started to scroll through her text messages. She found the one she was looking for and handed the phone back to Tom.

"Mom sent me this message by accident," Jessica claimed.

The text message read, "*H, looking forward to sailing with you to Vancouver this summer. You have really helped me get over my fear of the water. Love always, Syd.*"

Tom took a deep breath. Looking at the picture and reading the text message didn't just sting, it was devastating. For years he had begged Syd to go sailing with him. Supposedly she had tried phobia therapy and other potential cures to overcome her fear of the water, but with no success. Harold comes along and now she's suddenly just fine with sailing on the open ocean?

"I hate Harold, Dad. He's a completely boring, obnoxious jerk," Jessica announced.

"He's alright, but I don't like him being around the house all the time," Jonas added. "I don't like his stupid habit of making us breakfast. Fake bacon is gross. So are egg white omelets. I can't believe mom eats that crap."

Tom needed a minute. He excused himself and went to the restroom.

Tom's face was flushed. He was angry. Why? Because Sydney was with someone else? He knew that she was dating before her disclosure today. Sydney was a beautiful woman and although she was in her late forties, age had not done any damage to her looks.

As their sex life diminished over the years, Tom wondered if Syd fooled around on him. He never found any evidence of it that's for sure. Truth be told, despite her beauty and brains, Tom was just not attracted to Syd anymore. The spark, the flame that Tom was once certain would never go out between him and Sydney had slowly flickered out died.

Tom's brother told him that from a man's perspective getting and being divorced is an emotionally complicated process. As Gabriel put it, "The band has stopped playing, but you can still hear the music." While Syd was not his wife anymore, she would always in a very real sense be his wife. Ties so deep are not easily cut, if they ever truly are.

Looking in the mirror in the men's room Tom said silently to himself, I need to get out of here, out of California. I have to turn the page or I will go nuts. I need ocean therapy and lots of it.

Tom's kids were hurting. They were caught in the middle and no amount of money or counseling or expensive distractions could heal the wound created by their parents splitting. He took a few deep breaths, splashed more water on his face and went back to the table. Tonight was about Jonas and Jessica, not about him.

As he walked back into the main dining hall Tom took notice, as he always did, of the Palace Hotel's beautiful architecture. He and Syd had dinner here the first night they moved to San Francisco. Her parents were both alive back then and joined them for dinner. Jessica was barely two.

Tom and Syd were still in love ten years ago. In retrospect, signs of their growing estrangement were evident. Neither of them wanted to see the negative; they wanted everything to be perfect between them. So they both whitewashed issues rather than compromise and resolve them – Tom's unhappiness about having to leave San Diego and Sydney's feeling that Tom was not enthusiastic or supportive enough of her budding career as a writer being chief.

But Sydney wasn't here now. She was at home with Harold or talking with Harold on the phone making plans to go sailing. Stop it Tom, he chastised himself. Get a grip. Be there for your kids.

"Dad, the waitress wanted to know if you liked the wine. I took a taste and told her it was fine." Jonas said with a sly grin.

"Please tell me that's your idea of a bad joke," Tom said.

"Lighten up! Jeez!" Jonas said.

"As long as you pass all of your drug tests I'll lighten up," Tom said as he sat down and took a sip of his Chardonnay.

"How long do I have to keep getting tested? I've been clean for four months. It's not like I was an addict or something. It was just weed, Dad. It's basically legal anyway."

"It's legal if you're over twenty one. You're fifteen, remember? Drugs are not good for growing brains or for any brains for that matter," Tom said.

The food arrived. The kids loved going to dinner with their father because they could eat like kids eat when they were with him. Tom was not surprised when they ordered fried everything with maximum grease. They would be ordering dessert too, without a doubt.

"Dad, I really need a new computer. My laptop just isn't cutting it," Jess said, in between bites of fried shrimp, her favorite food.

"We just bought you a laptop six months ago. Has it stopped working?" Tom asked.

"No, but its old now; a phone or laptop older than six months is outdated," Jess argued.

"Keep using it, honey. You can do what you need to do on it, no doubt," Tom said.

"Harold said that he would buy me a new one, so you don't have to worry about it," Jessica said as she slipped her headphones back on.

Tom reached over and slid Jess' headphones off. "Put those away. We're talking, not listening to music." Jess groused a bit, but then set her headphones down.

"I think Harold and your mom might become a permanent thing. We all have to get used to the idea. I know this much, your mother would never bring anyone around you kids who was not a good person," Tom said.

"He's a jerk," Jessica whined. "I don't care how much stuff he buys me; he'll always be a jerk."

"Has he said something unkind to you? Or hurt you in some way?" Tom asked.

"No, he's sooo polite," Jess said sarcastically, "but he thinks he can just step in and be you. I don't like that, not at all. He's not my dad, you are."

"I'll always be your dad, honey. That will never change."

"But will you ever stand up to mom? She walks all over you. That affects me and Jess, you know that right?" Jonas said.

"Jonas, your mother does not 'walk all over me.' That's a rude thing to say about her and about me."

"Yes she does," Jessica added. "If you would have stood up to her a few times I'll bet you two would still be married."

"Alright, that's enough," Tom said. "Let's change the subject."

"Okay. When do we leave for Hawaii?" Jonas said.

"Harold has a dog. Mom says that when Harold comes to live with us the dog is coming too," Jessica announced.

"Eat," Tom said. He didn't have to be a psychologist to see that his kids were trying to bait him. They were in pain over all of this. They probably blamed themselves for the divorce, at least to some degree.

They didn't talk about Harold, Hawaii or the break-up for the rest of the meal. In fact, they didn't talk about much. Jess slid her headphones back on and Jonas started playing *Candy Crush* on his Android.

Tom ate and thought. While he felt guilty about his kids' unhappiness and he was still reeling from the revelations about Syd, whenever he took a deep breath and looked around Tom wasn't in the Palace, he was a thousand miles away in the Pacific, slowly making his way towards Hawaii.

Chapter Nine

"There he is," Tom said as he opened his front door and Gabriel Campbell stepped inside. "It's so good to see you." Since Gabriel moved to Denver from San Diego three years ago to practice environmental law, Tom rarely saw his older brother and his only sibling.

"Nice place you got here," Gabriel said as he tossed his luggage on the floor. "Everything a bachelor needs except for the eighty inch plasma TV. Where's that?"

"I have a small TV in the bedroom. The kids have a big screen upstairs. I'm not much of a television watcher."

"That's always been puzzling. You know how to stand and look and speak for the camera, yet you aren't interested in TV at all."

"A collection of paradoxes, that's me."

"It runs in the family. Our friends call us quirky. I like to think that idiosyncrasies are endearing," Gabriel said.

"Are you still watching every Dodger game?"

"Never miss one, especially now since they have more money than God and have purchased all the best players. You?"

"Nah, not so much anymore," Tom admitted. "Jonas is into longboarding and diving and sailing. It's not like when we were kids. Baseball isn't that important these days."

"Blasphemy. You can go to hell for saying things like that," Gabriel joked.

"I do have tickets for us this weekend. They cost a small fortune, but we have seats four rows behind the visitors' dugout. We might have to reconsider wearing Dodger hats to the game though. The fans at AT&T don't appreciate it."

"You got us tickets for all three games?" Gabriel asked hopefully.

"All three," Tom confirmed.

"When was the last time we went to a Dodger game?" Gabriel asked.

"Two years ago when I came to Denver. Coors Field. The Bums won 5 to 2," Tom said.

"Got a beer?" Gabriel asked.

"One Henie coming up," Tom said.

Gabriel and Tom spent a half an hour catching up on kids, life and careers. They avoided discussing the eight hundred pound elephant in the room, Tom's divorce, but after a while there was no more dodging the issue.

"So, is it final?" Gabriel did not need to define what "it" was, Tom knew.

"We signed the papers last week. The judge signs them tomorrow, I think. It's all over."

"Talk to me. I know this cannot be an easy time for you," Gabriel said as he popped the cap on another beer.

"Syd has a new man in her life. It sounds serious."

"I know people in low places. Broken legs or something more severe?" Gabriel joked.

"He is a good guy by all accounts. He's been nothing but polite to me the couple of times I've spoken with him on the phone."

"I freakin' hate him," Gabriel said.

"For God's sakes why?"

"Because you should. Everyone is supposed to hate their ex's new guy. It's required," Gabriel said.

"I like to think I'm a bit more mature than that, Gabe. Besides, I don't want to be with Syd. I don't know what I want, but I definitely do not want to be married to her any longer."

"Are we on Oprah or something? This is me you're talking to," Gabriel said.

"Sydney and I had something great once, but it's over. I guess it wasn't meant to last. We both love our kids. Life goes on."

"You need to get laid."

"Here we go…"

"Meaningless sex; it cures a lot of ills. Sure worked for me between door number one and Cynthia." Gabriel had been happily married to his second wife Cynthia for almost twenty years.

"No thanks. I'm not dead in that department, but casual sex does not interest me."

"Pull out your wallet and give it to me," Gabriel ordered.

"Give you what?"

"Your Man Club card. You're acting way too rational and reasonable about all this. Where is the fire, the indignation, the good old 'she's a crazy bitch' banter?"

Tom laughed. He knew Gabriel was kidding around, trying to cheer him up. Gabriel Campbell was actually far more conservative in almost every way than he was.

"I think I'm being a bad father. That bothers me a lot, Gabe."

"My nephew and niece love you. I talked with Jonas for half an hour last night," Gabriel said.

"Mind if I ask what he said?"

"More than anything else he is worried about you. He's afraid of you sailing to Hawaii on your own. He wants to be with you, to be there for you if something happens."

"He told you this?"

"Yes. After he told me about his latest exploits shooting heroin and robbing banks."

"Seriously, Gabriel."

"Yes he told me that. Why aren't you taking Jonas with you to Hawaii?"

"Syd thinks it's too dangerous for him to go with me. She has a valid argument. It's not like sailing around the bay. I won't go against her on this one."

"Okay, then who are you taking?"

"With me? No one, I'm going solo," Tom said.

"Okay, you can have your Man Club card back, but for heaven's sakes take someone with you; preferably a female half your age."

"I really need to just be alone, Gabe. The past year has been damn hard. I'm not sure who I am anymore and I don't like myself much right now."

"Been to Mass lately? Confession is good for the soul," Gabriel offered.

"I know you still go to church and good for you. Me, I need the cathedral of the ocean. I'd love to take Jonas with me, but maybe it's best for a lot of reasons if he stays here. Did he tell you that he might come to live with me in Hawaii?"

"He did," Gabriel said. "He thinks Sydney will get her way on that too and talk you out of it. I also think he feels like you might be happier living without him."

"He said that?"

"No, he didn't. It's just an impression I got that's all. Your son thinks you are the greatest guy in the world, other than his uncle Gabriel, of course."

"Jessica... I don't have a clue what's going on with her. Everything is a tragedy. The simplest things are complicated. She is always upset about something," Tom said.

"Jess is twelve. Hello," Gabriel said and then slugged down the rest of his beer.

"Meaning?"

"My three daughters have all become semi-competent and largely rational adults, but when they were twelve, thirteen, in there... Mother of God! You remember; it was insanity around my house. Twelve year old girls cry over anything and everything. They are demanding, irrational and generally belligerent."

Tom laughed. It was so good to have his brother with him again, even if it was only for a few days. Gabriel could always cheer him up, no matter what. Then it hit him, a great idea.

"Why don't you come with me? Tell the firm you need a thirty day hiatus. Let someone else battle the EPA this summer. Let's go sailing."

"I thought about that. I wish I could! I have a trial starting in three weeks. It's been postponed twice. I can't bail, it's not possible. Last summer would have been perfect! Why didn't you plan this a year ago!"

"It would have been a trip to remember forever," Tom said.

"I do have a request, Tom."

"Okay."

"I'm afraid I'm going to have to insist on it."

"I'm listening," Tom said.

"Whatever you do out there, don't get dead."

Chapter Ten

"I promise. I will not take a satellite phone, but -."

"Tom, it's a gift from me. I'll pay for the phone and three months' worth of service. There are no strings attached, you should know that," Sydney said.

"I do know that. A satellite phone is unnecessary. Take half that money and buy Jess a new laptop. Tell her it's from both of us."

"Without a satellite phone you will be out of touch for days at a time, maybe a couple of weeks. What if something happens, to the kids I mean, how would I -."

"Sydney, you need to get used to the idea that I am not going to be around anymore. I will be living in Hawaii."

"That's hard for me," Syd said, in a very sad tone.

"What about Harold? Isn't he living with you now?"

"He's around but… I'm not talking about Harold, I'm talking about you."

"This is where I say something really cute and cruel like, 'If you wanted me around why did you divorce me.'"

"I guess it hasn't really hit home until now. Not the divorce, the fact that I can't just call you and go to lunch or ask you to pick up the kids or rely on you to rescue me when my car dies."

"What did you think it would be like when we split up?" Tom paused and took a deep breath. "Sydney, I'm sorry. I'm not trying to be mean, not at all. I need some time to be alone. Can you appreciate that? My life has been torn apart. I'm sick to death of being a corporate goon. I don't know who I am anymore. I can't be a good father to the kids until I get my head together. You of all people should understand that, at least conceptually."

"You're not my client, you're my husband."

"I'm not you're husb -."

"Tell me I didn't just say that. I'm glad we aren't Skyping, because my face is totally red."

"Syd, please." Tom was trying his best to be empathetic, but it was just too much. "Sydney, you'll be fine. The kids will be fine. Once I get to Hawaii, I'll fly them both over for a couple of weeks before school starts. You know that I'm never going to stop being their father."

"They both love you more than they love me. That's the hard truth of it."

Tom moved the cell phone away from his ear. He was standing in the middle of his luggage, everything he was taking to the boat. The cab had arrived. The cab driver was walking towards his open front door, ready to help load the large pile of stuff and to deliver Tom and his bags to the marina.

"The cab is here. I've got to go," Tom said.

"Call me on the radio before you're out of range. Don't take any crazy chances. I want to say, to tell you …"

"I love you too, Syd. We aren't together anymore, but I will never stop loving you."

Tom only heard soft sobs before Sydney ended the call.

◊   ◊   ◊

"She's a beauty, sir, an absolutely outstanding boat. How old is she?"

Tom was busy checking his gear, so he was distracted when the guy from Stem to Stern Boat Service asked his question.

"I'm sorry, you asked me something?"

"How old is your sloop?"

"She was built in 1964. Damn near my age, almost exactly," Tom said.

"The OGs around here… oh sorry, I didn't mean to -."

"That's alright. I'm an OG; more of a curmudgeon than an OG, but what the hell."

"Thirty foot Rawsons are little tanks. People have sailed around the globe solo in these babies."

"I would not own another boat. This beauty and I go way back. I bought her in San Diego fifteen years ago," Tom said.

"As you asked, we inspected her. Not a crack or weak spot in the fiberglass. That's hard to believe after fifty years of service. I see that the engine has been replaced."

"Five years ago, yes. I also switched out all of the electronics and sails last year, but pretty much everything else other than the propane galley heater is original equipment. Can we review the stores?"

"Yes sir," the man said as he looked at his clipboard.

Tom and the man reviewed what had been brought on board. Food, fresh water, linens, cleaning supplies, dive gear, spare main sail – everything Tom needed to be safe and comfortable for thirty days at sea.

"How many propane tanks did you bring aboard?" Tom asked.

"Four. That should be more than enough. Assuming you passed through the coldest weather ever recorded in the Pacific in July and you took six weeks to get there, you'd still have a tank or more to spare."

"And are they secure?" Tom asked.

"All of them are strapped down in the propane locker aft of the cockpit. Wanna take a look?" the man asked.

"Nah, I'll just check them off my list. What about the new lines? You switched them all out?"

"Every line on the boat is now brand new, just as you specified."

Tom took a minute to review his list one last time. If anything was missing, he would have to do without it. There were no marinas between here and Hawaii, only open water.

"Good enough then," Tom said. He signed the paperwork.

"Leaving today?" the man asked as he was climbing out of the cabin.

"No, at first light," Tom said. "I want to sail through the Golden Gate at dawn."

"Sounds like a plan. If you need anything else, just give me a call on the cell. We're around until eight p.m. or so."

"Will do. Thanks," Tom said.

Two weeks ago Tom moved his boat from Richmond, just up the river in the northwest part of the bay, to its present location near Fisherman's Wharf. It was expensive to park the boat here even for a short time, but Tom wanted everything to be perfect.

For the past year he had done his best to prepare for his adventure. He had taken three extended sailing trips of several days each – two going south, the other one to Oregon and back. While he had never sailed solo for 2000 plus miles, a journey he would be starting in the morning, he was confident in his skills.

He could not make the trip in a better boat. For decades Ron Rawson built some of the world's finest sailboats. He built them for cruising and he built them to last with good, old fashioned craftsmanship. Because Rawson built his sailboats primarily for use in the cold and rough waters of the Pacific Northwest, they were ideal for tropical cruising as well.

The boat was the perfect size for a solo sail – not too big and not too small. Its thirty foot hull could cut through all but the roughest of seas with ease. If the wind died, the sloop could motor along for days at a slow but steady pace. The berth was six feet six inches tall with plenty of elbow room. In fact, Tom preferred the boat's bed over the expensive mattress he had at home. The small head was more than adequate with a toilet, sink, shower and plenty of storage. The galley was very nice; the refrigerator was a bit larger than the norm.

For the first time in a long time Tom felt comfortable. He shut off his cell phone. It would remain off for the next month barring an emergency. From this point on, Tom vowed, no more distractions, no more world. He wanted to be alone with his thoughts and the occasional symphony he would pipe through the boat's sound system.

As he sat at his galley table, he looked across at the pictures hanging on the wall. He hadn't changed them in years; Syd standing on the bow the day he bought her, the kids at various ages – Jonas was born two months before he bought the boat. The photos were a recording of his family history.

Both Jonas and Jessica loved to sail with their father, but Jonas more so. Tom's passion for sailing had been passed down to his son. When Jonas came to Hawaii to live with him, Tom planned on buying him a Hobie Cat and teaching him to sail on his own.

Not only had Tom not taken Sydney's pictures down from the wall, he also had no intention of renaming the boat.

Her name was Sydney and it always would be.

Chapter Eleven

Tom got up at five a.m. and dressed in jeans, deck shoes, a collared shirt and a windbreaker. He made himself coffee and ate a bowl of cereal. He switched on the radio and tuned it to the classical music station. Soon he would be out of reach of any FM radio signal. He spent an hour or so preparing Sydney for departure.

With Vanhal's symphony in G minor gently flowing through the speakers, Tom untied his lines and slowly motored out of the marina. The sea was calm and the air still, but once he reached the Farallon Islands the forecast was for a steady fifteen knot breeze. The sun was just peeking over the Oakland hills on the eastern horizon. Alcatraz was to his starboard – the early morning sunlight was dancing off the old prison walls. Tiburon, a city he often visited in his boat to eat lunch or just to perch for an afternoon by the bay, was to his north.

Tom moved into the channel, maneuvering around a cargo vessel that was putting into port. Once he reached the Golden Gate the air was salty and fresh. He filled his lungs with the sea breeze.

Rather than being stressed or concerned about one issue or another, all Tom was thinking about was when he could start sailing. The wind picked up as soon as he cleared the harbor. He opened his sail and turned off his engine. Within a minute or so he was nicely making way at a steady five knot pace.

He wanted to spend his first day, maybe two, sailing around the Farallons. This time of year a variety of whale species visited the islands. Tom had never seen any sperm whales there, but he had seen plenty of orcas, greys and humpbacks. With a sailboat it was sometimes possible to get close to the whales because there was no engine noise to frighten them away.

Whenever he visited the Farallons Tom thought about Henry. He knew that by now, if he had survived, Henry would be a mature sperm whale, fifty to sixty feet long and would weigh in excess of forty tons. He would be eating almost a ton of food every day. Very likely Henry would be roaming around the Pacific – maybe north towards Alaska in the summer and then back to California in the wintertime.

While nothing could match the joy Tom felt watching his children being born, his day spent with Henry on the beach was a life changing event. It was such a unique experience that Tom felt it could not be compared or categorized with anything else. Even though it had been twenty years, when Tom closed his eyes he could see Henry lying in the sand looking both impressive and helpless at the same time.

As he neared the Farallons the wind picked up. Tom was now moving at a seven knot clip and the seas were frothy. Sydney cut through the foot and half chop almost effortlessly. For a moment he thought about Jonas. Yes, it would have been wonderful to be with him out here, they had sailed to the Farallons a few times before, but he had to admit that solitude was incredible.

He saw the orcas first. There was a pod of them, at least seven whales that he could count. They were swimming together, no doubt searching for food in the form of a stray seal or sea lion. They swam around and under Tom's boat as he reached the northernmost island.

There were sea birds here by the thousands – gulls, puffins, Cassin's auklets and many other species. The entire area was a

National Marine Sanctuary. Oddly enough, the islands themselves were still officially part of the city of San Francisco. When the city boomed in the nineteenth century, the islands were a seemingly endless source of food for the residents. In the 1850s and 60s San Franciscans took as many as half a million sea bird eggs a month to feed themselves, along with a large number of seals and sea lions. But since the beginning of the twentieth century, starting with the Executive Order issued by Theodore Roosevelt in 1909, the islands and their wildlife have been protected by the United States government.

Tom saw the humpbacks next, two of them, a mother and her calf. They were about half mile away when he first spotted them, but he was able to angle Sydney in for a closer look.

They were massive creatures, yet they moved through the water with such grace. Tom thought this is what Henry and his mother must have looked like back in '95 before the cow's collision with the cruiser. For almost two hours Tom stayed with the pair as they slowly made their way around the islands. Then, just before sunset, they dipped below the waves and they were gone.

Tom set his anchor on the leeward side of Southeast Farallon Island. It is the only inhabited island in the chain. As if on cue, as soon as the sun set the wind died down. It was warm, by Northern California standards, almost sixty degrees. Tom lit the stove and cooked himself an omelet. He had to eat all of his perishable food first and since he had more than two dozen eggs omelets, toast and coffee made a perfect meal.

Off in the distance he could hear the sound of humpback whales singing. Unlike Henry's clicks, the humpbacks produced haunting melodies almost in the form of notes, much like a whale symphony. Tom had heard them singing once before on a previous trip here, but he knew that it was special to be blessed with the opportunity to listen to them again. They called to each other for an hour as Tom sat on his deck listening.

Around ten Tom retired. He switched on the small light in his berth. He brought along a book to read on his trip, Melville's classic *Moby Dick*. He'd read the novel before, but it had been over twenty five years since he'd done so.

The story was like an old friend. He imagined himself being a whaler a hundred and fifty years ago in New England. He could definitely relate to Captain Ahab in at least in one respect – he was also fascinated by a particular sperm whale.

When he turned off the light and closed his eyes to go to sleep, Tom saw Henry as he saw him last, spinning in the water and swimming away after he had been rescued.

Chapter Twelve

Tom decided to leave the Farallons the next day. He could have easily spent another day there, even a week, but they were not his destination. He was sailing to Hawaii. The excitement of beginning his journey across the Pacific outweighed the appeal of familiar territory.

Before he left the Farallons, Tom saw a couple of grey whales swimming in the distance. These creatures were even larger than sperm whales. He had never seen one up close, but that would have to wait for another day. He was headed southwest, the greys were moving north.

The wind was cooperating, so Tom was able to move along at a steady six knot clip. Three other sailboats were also headed in his general direction and for a couple of hours Tom wondered if he would have some company on his trip to Hawaii, but mid-afternoon they turned and tacked back towards California.

Now Tom was where he always wanted to be, alone on the Pacific sailing towards the tropics. He could see nothing around him but blue water. He knew that many people, perhaps most people, would be scared to death to be out on the ocean all by themselves. While he was not ignorant of the potential dangers, he was overwhelmed by the beauty and serenity of the experience.

For the first time in his life, Tom was truly disconnected from the rest of the planet. He was now out of range of anything except for his ship to shore radio and soon even that would be useless until he neared Hawaii. With every mile of ocean he crossed, Tom felt more relaxed. His mind was liberated. He allowed his thoughts to wander wherever they wanted to go.

Last month Tom celebrated his fiftieth birthday. Jonas and Jessica made a big deal of it. He shared cake and gifts with them at his condo. He put on a happy face for his children and made the day about them, not about him. But when he dropped them off at Syd's house later that evening Tom did not go straight home. He went to a bar he knew well on Union Street and sat down to have a couple of drinks.

Tom wasn't feeling sorry for himself, not exactly. He was very aware how fortunate he was, and in so many ways. Tom was a casual drinker at best; he was not there to get drunk, only to reflect for a few minutes and for a change of scenery before he went home for the night.

As he sat on his stool sipping his Glenlivet, Tom considered his good fortune. How many people in this room, in the city for that matter, could say that they were basically set for life financially? While he was not rich, at least by his definition of rich, Tom knew that after the divorce he would be worth in excess of a couple of million bucks. Most of his net worth was liquid, or soon would be once the house was sold or refinanced.

He was in great health and decent physical condition. While he was not the gym rat that he once was, he vowed to work out at least four days per week from this point on. He still had his hair, for which he was very thankful. From the occasional glances and even stares he got from women, he figured that he had not yet reached the stage of being totally invisible to the opposite sex.

His children were great – not perfect, but budding human beings on their way to becoming what he hoped were two happy adults. He knew that he had to re-focus on being a better father, but he gave himself some credit in the parent department.

He tried to be a good dad because he loved his kids. Was that enough? He asked himself.

As Tom drank and listened to the blues music, he watched as a couple that were about his age or perhaps a little younger walk into the bar and sit at a table. They were clearly very into each other – touching hands and looking into each other's eyes. They were in love, but Tom noticed that there were no rings on their fingers.

He assumed that they were still dating and not yet married. How long had they been a couple, he wondered. Would they stay together? He knew that the odds were at best 50-50 that they would go the distance. And even if they did remain married all of their lives, would they be happy? What was "happy" when it came to marriage? Was staying married in the twenty first century just too difficult of a proposition?

The truth was Tom missed not only being in love, but even more so having a companion. Sydney had ceased being his companion years ago. She was a fantastic business partner and a great mother, but the intimacy they once took for granted had just faded away. Tom knew that he was as much, or more, to blame for that than Sydney was.

Tom finished his Scotch and went home. He watched a few minutes of the late show on TV and went to sleep. He was happy as hell that his fiftieth birthday was over.

The sun was getting lower on the horizon. It was time to stop for the night. There was no place to drop anchor here, unless the anchor had thousands of feet of chain. So Tom took down his sail and dropped a sea anchor. The sea anchor would keep his boat from drifting too far off course during the night.

The second dinner of his trip was a hamburger. Tom knew that he should probably not eat burgers, but he loved them.

The stove sprang to life on command. Most of the boat was powered by a diesel engine, directly or indirectly. The engine recharged the batteries and it also ran the main heater, if heat was required. But the stove was a propane burner as was a small space heater in the galley. Tom installed the galley heater because most of the time it was simply a waste of diesel to heat both the berth and main cabin; the small propane heater was usually all that he needed.

As the meat sizzled in the pan, Tom pulled out one of his duffels. Inside was a plastic box. Inside the box was unopened mail.

Tomorrow, he vowed, I'll get to that.

After eating and securing Sydney for the night, Tom went to bed. There was no need for an alarm clock. When he got up, he got up. He might get underway at dawn or not until noon. Out here he was free to make choices, to do what he wanted to do when he wanted to do it.

Chapter Thirteen

Tom's parents were not wealthy. His father was a journeyman carpenter who worked mostly on industrial sites, often on marine projects. He was a veteran of the Second World War and a "Humphrey Bogart" type of guy. He drank beer and smoked cigarettes. While the beer did him no harm, the smokes did. Lance Campbell died of lung cancer in 1981.

A year before his death Lance took his two sons, Gabriel and Tom, to Hawaii. Lance had been to Pearl Harbor once during the war on his way to fight the Japanese, but he had not been back to Hawaii since. Lance was not a hundred percent physically; he suspected that that there was something wrong with him, but the cancer had yet to be diagnosed.

They visited Oahu, but they spent most of their three week vacation on the Big Island, on the dry side. They rented a condo and snorkeled every day. Still in high school, Tom was already in love with the water – he spent most of his free time in San Diego either diving or surfing. Gabriel was in college, a year away from graduation. While Gabe liked the ocean, he was not as crazy about it as his brother was.

On the trip, Tom's father took his boys deep sea fishing. They caught Ahi and Ono and had a great time with their dad, but the highlight of the fishing excursion for Tom was the whales. Humpbacks were numerous in the waters off Hawaii in the summer. This was the first time he had seen a humpback up close.

For a year or so after his trip to Hawaii Tom read everything he could about whales. After graduation, he enrolled at UC San Diego majoring in Marine Biology. He envisioned himself becoming the next Jacques Cousteau, traveling around the world on an expensive, ultra sleek dive boat making underwater documentaries and exploring the sea.

How long it's been since I've had those dreams, Tom thought as he sailed. Somewhere along the way Jacques Cousteau got replaced by Jacques Paycheck. One thing led to another. Tom gravitated toward the communications end of the scientific career spectrum. This move was also initially made with grandiose intent – he had to have a great on camera presence if he was going to dazzle the viewing audience as he recounted the details of his latest deep sea adventure.

When it came time to join the real world after getting his college degree, Tom's options were limited. The Cousteau people simply were not hiring. So he went to UCLA and got his Master's degree in communications. He never gave up his love for the ocean, but now he reasoned that his entry into marine science might have to be made through the back door.

Scripps was hiring when Tom finished his program at UCLA. He created a clever video portfolio of himself as a faux public relations rep for a made up major marine institution. Scripps was impressed by Tom's burning desire to work for them, his media savvy and undergrad background in marine science. Over five hundred people competed for the entry level job Tom won to become the lowest person on the totem pole in the public relations department at Scripps.

I still had my dreams back then, Tom thought as he adjusted his heading to stay on course. When I lost my dreams, part of me died too. The winds were stronger today so he was making great time. The only sound Tom heard was the gentle thumping of the waves against the bow as Sydney continued on her southwest course.

Tom didn't lose his dreams as much as he kept postponing them. He rose quickly through the ranks at Scripps and was fortunate to benefit from a number of timely retirements. Within a few years he was promoted to the head of the public relations department. He was making six figures.

When he met Sydney Rogers, Tom was thinking about leaving Scripps and joining a film crew. It would have been a huge step down in terms of pay, but the documentary film company wanted Tom to be their on air voice for a cable television series about sharks. Just as he had a few years earlier when he took a job at Scripps, Tom had romantic ideas about where this job might lead him. Suddenly, becoming Jacques Cousteau was back in the picture.

Sydney changed all that.

When Tom met Syd he fell in love, for the first and only time in his life. Literally from the instant he met her, his priorities, his dreams, changed. He still wanted to be Jacques Cousteau, but now that goal would have to be accomplished within a marriage. He went from thinking about leaving San Diego for Los Angeles and a spot on a globetrotting film crew to how he might swing a down payment on a larger home and deciding which engagement ring to buy.

Tom never told Syd about the job he turned down with the film crew. She was his life now and all he wanted to do was make her happy. Living his life for her was personally fulfilling for Tom, at least for a time. When the kids came along, Tom fell in love all over again. Having children was a miraculous, wonderful thing.

Looking back, Tom could clearly see the turning point in his marriage. Sydney wanted to move back to San Francisco, her home town. Her writing career was taking off – she was making a name for herself as a nationally known addiction/recovery guru. With Tom's help and coaching, Sydney was now very comfortable in front of the camera and the camera certainly loved her.

The economics of the decision were straightforward. Sydney was making in excess of $350,000 per year with the potential to make much more. For many reasons, it was better for her career to live in Northern California. At the same time Syd was pushing Tom to move, Pioneer Insurance reached out to Tom through one of Sydney's publishing connections. They made him a very attractive offer to be their chief spokesperson.

Sydney denied being behind the job offer from Pioneer, but the timing seemed more than convenient to Tom. He certainly would not have been angry with her if she was, except that she was using the job offer as an incentive to get Tom to agree to live in San Francisco. Tom did not want to leave San Diego.

At the same time Sydney made her desire known to leave So Cal, Tom was considering approaching his wife with a bold idea. A friend of his from Scripps, an oceanographer, was set to receive a huge government grant within six months to research climate change. A decade earlier climate change was a very new and hot topic. The grant was huge, five million plus, and it was being matched by a similar amount of funding from the private sector.

Tom's friend wanted Tom on board as the face and voice of the new firm. In addition to his media/PR duties, Tom would also be given a role in the field. That meant that Tom could spend considerable time on the water, perhaps as much as two months a year.

I should have told Syd about that opportunity, Tom thought. Replaying the events in his mind, and he hadn't really thought about this in depth for years, this was when their intimacy really began to disintegrate. Rather than discussing each other's hopes and dreams, Tom just said yes to Sydney. She was delighted, he was deflated. This was the beginning of a serious resentment Tom would build towards his wife over the coming years.

While Syd would probably have said no, Tom did not give her the chance to say yes. Tom knew that wasn't fair to Sydney.

While he was a man with few regrets, the regrets he did have were substantial.

But now when Tom thought about the what ifs he did so with a different perspective. The ocean cleared his mind and opened his heart. Life is not lived through a rear view mirror; it is lived moving forward one day at a time.

Hawaii was ahead for Tom, along with a chance to rekindle his old dreams, at least to some degree. The Hawaii Institute of Marine Biology was not the Cousteau Society, but Tom wasn't chasing that dream anymore. He wanted to get back into the marine world, but he also wanted to be a father to his kids.

Tom smiled. He was thankful that he was out here on the water, grateful that even after a few days he was already feeling much more comfortable in his own skin. This trip was exactly what he needed at just the right time.

As sunset approached, he lowered his sail. The wind was brisk, so the sea would likely provide a swaying bed for the night. Tom was looking forward to that. Being rocked to sleep by the waves had a very definite appeal.

Chapter Fourteen

The days seemed to run together now. Tom's new routine was far simpler than the one he had back in California – get up whenever, but usually no later than seven thirty or so, start the coffee and make a simple breakfast. Check the satellite weather information system to be sure that he wasn't sailing into something foul, raise the sail and keep moving towards Hawaii.

Tom had been blessed with near perfect weather conditions. The wind was just enough at twenty knots or so to propel Sydney along at a nice clip. So far, the storms were staying to the north. As he moved south, the weather got warmer. Temperatures in the daytime now approached seventy five degrees. He gave up his jeans for shorts, his collared shirt for a t-shirt.

At night when he stopped to eat and sleep Tom would sometimes read, sometimes listen to music and occasionally tap into his plastic box. Inside the box were a variety of items – unopened mail, old letters, legal documents, his resume and professional background papers, video clips of him that needed to be transferred to digital and electronically filed according to some yet to be devised semi-cogent system and a couple of old style paper photo albums.

Because he did not have a place to live yet on Oahu other than his boat, Tom left all of his furniture and ninety five percent of his belongings in the condo. When he got a place on land, although part of him kept arguing that he could just as easily live on the boat, he planned on flying back to San Francisco, packing everything up and shipping it to the islands.

For whatever reason, "just because" being paramount, tonight was the night he chose to go through some unopened mail.

He really didn't want to think too much about his fiftieth birthday. Yes, Tom admitted to himself as he sipped his black tea and opened the box, that was silly. But silly or not, it was real.

In one sense age is just a number but in another sense, which was far more important to Tom at the moment, age represented a ticking clock on his dreams. He was no longer twenty five, full of endless energy and wild imaginings. He missed the freedom of those days and while if he had it to do all over again he would marry Syd if for no other reason than it meant Jonas and Jessica were in the world, he wanted to be young and free and full of promise again.

He had only opened five birthday cards from the more than a hundred he had received. He started to go through them now, carefully placing the ones he'd reviewed in a neat pile that would soon become part of the boat's trash. Through his job at Pioneer, Tom met and regularly interacted with some important, high profile people. His cards reflected his old profession.

The mayor of San Francisco, well not the mayor personally but one of his staff, sent him a card that appeared to be personalized but was in fact cookie cutter. The Congressman from his district sent his best wishes. And so on...

Tom missed his kids. He knew that he would. If he didn't miss them, then something was wrong. He knew that they were missing him too, especially Jonas. He wondered how angry his son would be at him for not taking him along on the trip. He guessed that whatever anger Jonas was feeling it would pass, especially when he brought him out to Hawaii.

For sure Jonas was coming to live with him. Tom would simply not back down from that happening no matter what Syd said. In general, while it was more his fault than hers that he almost always gave into her, Tom was resolved to be more emotionally honest and firm with Sydney from now on. Not to be cruel, but to be genuine. She needed to understand that the old Tom who gave into almost every request she made had been reborn.

The Pacific had taken Tom Campbell into her arms and cocooned him, and given him the time required to transform. When he arrived in Hawaii in many ways Tom knew that he would not be the same man. He wanted to emerge as someone who was more confident, more whole and better able to make decisions.

Chapter Fifteen

Tom woke up, looked out the porthole in his berth and saw a dead calm sea. There was not a breath of wind. This was new – until now he had always enjoyed at least a light breeze every morning and stronger winds in the afternoon.

Maybe I'll sit here and let Sydney drift for a while Tom thought as he rose, put on his shorts, shoes, hat and T shirt and went out on deck. The sun was rising over the water; the first sliver of bright yellow was peaking over the blue.

There was nothing like sunrise at sea. Tom thought about all the sunrises on the ocean that he had enjoyed before. All of them before this trip were close to shore, so the sun was rising over the land. Not here. There was no land, only water. The incredible beauty of the morning stirred his soul again, just as it had done every morning for the past two weeks.

Before he went to bed last night Tom calculated his position. He was almost exactly halfway between San Francisco and Hawaii. The first half of his trip had taken him fifteen days, just about on schedule. While a part of him was interested in seeing dry land soon, most of Tom was perfectly content to remain on his boat indefinitely.

Smiling, Tom opened the valves on the propane tank from the cockpit. He heard a splash starboard. A pod of dolphins was circling Sydney, checking her out. After five minutes or so, they'd seen enough and they headed west, probably for the Hawaiian Islands Tom guessed.

As he headed below to make breakfast, Tom decided to fry up the last of his eggs and toast some bread in the oven. His supply of perishable food was nearly gone, so the eggs would be his last fresh treat for a couple of weeks. The coffee pot was electric. Tom switched it on. The stove and the oven were propane. Tom hadn't used the propane stove or oven much so far on the trip, maybe four or five times, the last being five days ago. When he needed to heat something up or cook, his small microwave was much faster and more convenient. It hadn't been nearly cold enough to fire up the propane galley heater.

The propane tanks on deck fed a gas line that led to the stove and oven. The line to the oven had a small leak. Since the beginning of the voyage, each time Tom opened the valve on the propane tank a small amount of propane leaked out. Since propane is heavier than air and there was no ventilation in this space, the gas had nowhere to go but to settle and pool in the bottom of the bilge. During the few minutes Tom was on deck watching the dolphins, enough propane had pooled to become a bomb.

Tom lit a match to light the oven. He wasn't paying too close attention to what he was doing; rather he was thinking about how he would spend his day. Maybe I'll finish *Moby Dick*. It might be time to polish my presentation for the Institute, Tom thought. Like it or not, sooner rather than later the real world is going to intrude on my solitude...

In the space below the oven, a tongue of gas from the propane pool in the bilge was drawn up towards the burner. When Tom moved the match towards the hole in the bottom of the oven, the tongue of gas ignited and sent flame racing towards the propane pool.

The explosion blew a hole through the hull at the keel. Tom was blown against the cabin ceiling and knocked unconscious. Because of the shape of the space between the stove and the hull, most of the blast was directed into the hull. Sydney was totally destroyed.

When Tom woke up his ribs felt like he had been kicked by a mule. His side hurt so much he could barely breathe. The cabin was more than halfway full of water. He was dazed and unsure just what had happened, but from the ringing in his ears and the destruction all around him he knew that had just lived through a huge explosion.

After he moved some light debris off of him, Tom looked out the porthole. He saw water. Then he became fully aware that he was sinking. Survival instincts kicked in. I have to get out of here now! Tom took a deep breath and then coughed and bent over in pain. His injury made taking in a huge gulp of air excruciating. But he breathed deeply a couple more times and the pain decreased. He took one last deep breath and went underwater.

The only way out of the sinking cabin appeared to be through a gaping hole where the stove once was. Tom saw deep blue through the hole and sunlight streaking through the water. Rather than go back up into the cabin and take another breath, Tom swam out of the hole. He assumed that he was only a few feet underwater.

He was wrong.

When Tom reached open water he saw the surface above him – thirty feet away. What was left of the cabin was sinking fast. Not yet within fifteen feet of the surface, Tom was out of breath. He closed his eyes and kicked and paddled for all he was worth. By the time he hit the surface, the only thing keeping Tom conscious was the searing pain in his chest.

He took in a huge gulp of air which was both incredibly relieving and mind numbingly painful. I'm not going to stay conscious long, Tom thought in panic. He looked around him and saw a six by six foot piece of the fiberglass hull lying in the water. Tom managed to pull himself up onto the fiberglass. Then he passed out.

When Tom woke up it was nearing sunset. The sun was on the other side of the horizon from where he last saw it. For a few seconds Tom was not sure where he was. Did I fall asleep lying on the deck? Maybe I better go inside; I'm probably burnt to a crisp... Then he remembered the explosion and the desperate swim to the surface. When he tried to move, his ribs reminded him that he was hurt. He still had his shorts on, but his shirt, hat and shoes were gone.

He looked at his chest and expected to see a terrible wound. There was some bruising, but no pooling of blood. He stretched a bit, which hurt but was not as painful as he thought it might be. With any luck at all I only have a deep bruise, Tom said. He was mildly relieved.

He sat up on his makeshift fiberglass raft and looked around. He was in the middle of a debris field. What was left of his beloved Sydney was floating all around him. Think, Tom, think. It will be dark soon. What am I looking for? The red emergency packs! They float too! Tom scanned the water in all directions. After a couple of minutes, he saw what he thought might be an emergency pack, but he wasn't sure. It was floating amidst other debris.

It took almost fifteen minutes to reach the red object. When Tom got to where he was going, he was not disappointed. He pulled the red emergency pack onto his raft and out of a clump of burnt rope and what was probably singed sail.

Inside the pack was five days' worth of food and water rations for one person, a first aid kit, an emergency blanket, a flare gun and a few other small items. The kit was designed to be used with a survival raft. Tom was fairly certain that his survival raft, which was stored un-inflated under the main mast, was sitting on the bottom of the Pacific.

Tom opened the emergency pack and grabbed one of the bottles of water. He gulped most of it down in seconds and reached for another. Wait, Tom told himself. Don't drink your water all at once. Who knows how long I'll be out here until help arrives. There were a few sips of water left in his first bottle and Tom finished them off. He took out an energy bar and ate it.

He found a few more barbequed sail pieces in the water and pulled them on to his raft. Then he balled them up and made a crude pillow. He pulled the emergency blanket over himself. He felt surprisingly chilly although Tom knew that it had to be over seventy degrees outside.

The sun was fully set. The night sky lit up before Tom's eyes. Tom loved looking at the stars at night on the open ocean. Lying on his back, he thought about the night before when he lay on the bow of Sydney doing the same thing, gazing up at the heavens.

His boat was gone. He had very few supplies. He was probably two hundred miles or more away from any major shipping lanes. No one was expecting him for fourteen days, at a minimum, in Honolulu. While Syd might start to worry if he did not reach out to her by radio in ten days or so when he was scheduled to be in radio range of Hawaii, she would likely not immediately hit the panic button when she didn't hear from him.

His marvelous adventure had become a nightmare. As he drifted off to sleep, the only thought that brought Tom comfort was that Jonas was not out here with him.

Chapter Sixteen

"Happy birthday," Syd said. All she had on was a skimpy white nightie.

"I wish everyday was my birthday," Tom said as he leaned back on the bed, propped himself up on a pillow and put his hands behind his head.

Moving to the dresser, Syd switched on the stereo. Harry Connick, Jr. now filled their bedroom with his smooth, crooner voice. Into the moment, Sydney smiled at her husband as she edged closer to the bed.

"The kids?" Tom asked.

"Janice has them. They're spending the night with her," Sydney said. "I'm afraid you're stuck with me."

"Come here," Tom said as he popped up and took Sydney in his arms.

Off in the distance Tom could hear squeaking or chirping. He thought it might be a phone or an alarm clock or maybe a stove timer. He couldn't do what he wanted to do, which was to give Sydney the attention she so richly deserved, until he shut off that damn noise. Syd couldn't hear it, or she didn't seem to care, but it was driving him crazy.

When he went to sit up, he felt the bed and it seemed rock hard; the mattress had a slick, plastic surface. His arms and legs were warm - not warm, hot. Then Syd was gone. Where did she go? Where am I?

Tom was still floating on the fiberglass hull piece in the middle of the Pacific. From the position of the sun in the sky, Tom guessed it had to be mid-morning. He had been dreaming, but it had seemed so real. Usually Tom's dreams were not so vivid, but this time... he truly regretted waking up before he finished what he started.

The chirping sound was coming from a pod of dolphins that were moving past him in the water. Tom looked at them with envy. They were gliding through the dark blue water effortlessly, completely unconcerned that they were hundreds of miles from land. They did not need the land to sustain them; the ocean provided everything they required. The ocean was their home.

Until yesterday, Tom was as comfortable as the dolphins were on the water. His beautiful boat, his water home, his prized Sydney, was now nothing but flotsam. He took a second to scan the horizon. The debris field was diffuse. It stretched mostly to the southeast, no doubt following the current.

There was no wind to move the scattered remnants of his boat. The sea was dead calm. It looked like he was floating on a giant backyard swimming pool. Only this pool was ten thousand feet deep and there was no patio to sit on and no sliding doors let him back inside the house.

Think Tom, think. As he gathered himself he remembered that he had fresh water, it was in the floating emergency pack. He looked around his makeshift raft. No pack. Where had it gone? If I've lost the pack...

Tom looked in all directions. The intense glare created from sunlight striking flat water was nearly blinding. He had to squint and hold his hand over his eyes to be able to scan the water effectively. Finally, he saw it. The red pack was perhaps twenty yards away, floating with other debris. He was certain that he had put the pack on the raft last night before he fell asleep. He also remembered sleeping under an emergency blanket and using a wadded up pile of old sail as a headrest. Those items were also nowhere to be seen.

The only conclusion he could reach while he was paddling towards the red emergency pack was that he must have thrashed around in the night and kicked or shoved it off the raft in his sleep. He vowed to be more careful. If the wind had been up the emergency pack might have drifted too far away to retrieve. If he lost his only source of fresh water and food he knew that he was doomed.

It took him nearly an hour to reach the emergency pack. Along the way he collected a couple of useful things – two pieces of sail, both five feet by ten feet or so and a three foot by eight inch piece of wood he assumed was from his former galley table, which he now used as an oar.

For the next six hours Tom paddled around the debris field looking in general for anything useful, but specifically for any of the other emergency packs. He found a blue baseball hat and a couple of pieces of shirts that had managed to free themselves from the captivity of a dresser drawer before the main cabin sank. One of the partial shirts, a red and white tee with *Coca Cola* written across the front, immediately became a head bandana and the hat went over it. Now at least his head and neck were shielded from the sun.

As the sun was about to set Tom stopped paddling around. He might resume his search tomorrow or then again maybe not. He assumed that everything had drifted in the same direction and he had reached what he thought was the end of the debris field. For all he knew, the other emergency packs had disintegrated in the explosion.

The explosion, Tom thought as he sipped from his precious fresh water bottle. How could I have been so stupid? He had not checked the propane tanks and lines. He assumed they were sound. The leak was slow so the gas sank and pooled undetected in the bilge. He never smelled the gas, but it was certainly there.

Because of his carelessness he was floating in the middle of the sea with nothing but a few days' supply of fresh water and food standing between him and certain death.

He wondered what Jonas and Jessica were doing right now. They were probably at home lounging around with one screen or another in their hands. Tom worried that his kids were addicted to screens – smart phones, tablets, televisions; they were always looking at some device. Jessica more than Jonas for sure; she and her *i Phone* were never apart.

When Tom was a kid growing up in Pasadena the world was a different place. There were five channels on the TV back then – cable television didn't become widely available until he left for college. After school and homework were done, Tom usually grabbed a mitt or basketball and headed out to play with the neighborhood boys. Pick-up games were everything. He imagined himself being Steve Garvey or Ron Cey or Dusty Baker making great plays in the field at Dodger Stadium or hitting a fastball for a home run over the left field wall and into the pavilion. If it was a basketball game he was playing, then he was Jerry West or Wilt Chamberlain scoring forty points against the Celtics in the NBA Finals.

Tom worried that his kids didn't do enough with other kids. Jonas was an avid long boarder, but that was a solo activity done with perhaps two or three other boys who were riding alongside him. Jessica hated sports of all kinds. The most exercise she got was walking home from the bus stop. She had a couple of close friends, but she almost never did things with groups of girls.

Have I done enough for them? Tom asked himself. Their college funds were huge and they also had large personal trust funds. But money wasn't everything, and Tom knew it. Have I taken every opportunity to try and help them? Have I loved on them as best as I could?

When I get back I have to do more, be a better dad, especially now after the divorce. I'll take Jessica with me to the gym, Jonas and I will go to Yellowstone like we had always planned to do....

Then he opened his eyes. The sun was nearly set. He looked around without difficulty now, the glare was gone.

"I'll never see them again," Tom said aloud. "I'm going to die out here."

For the next hour, he cried as the sky went from light to darkness. There was no moon so the world was black, illuminated only by the stars which were on magnificent display.

The inevitability of his fate now weighed heavily on his soul. He was a dead man; it was only a matter of time. He knew that the only human beings in the area were 36,000 feet above him in commercial airliners traveling at 500 miles per hour.

He had no idea what he could possibly do to improve his situation. He was totally alone and utterly helpless.

Chapter Seventeen

Tom slept in fits and starts that night, his second night on the water. His ribs were hurting like hell, but that was not his biggest concern. He'd bruised ribs before as a kid playing football and he knew that as long as he had not broken a rib, and he couldn't be certain that he hadn't but it didn't feel like he did, then it was just pain.

"I won't live long enough for my ribs to heal," Tom said aloud.

All night long Tom battled with the idea that there was absolutely no hope for his situation. By nature he was an optimist, but the years had sapped some of his innate positive spirit. For the past decade plus Tom had felt trapped. Granted his cage was a beautiful house on the hill, a 400 square foot office overlooking downtown San Francisco and a Mercedes Benz S500 sedan, but it was a cage nonetheless.

Now he had unwillingly traded his luxurious prison on land for a small piece of fiberglass floating in the middle of the ocean. If he slid off this small chunk of his former boat's hull and into the water he would last only an hour or so before his energy would run out and he would sink into the deep and drown and become part of the food chain.

As the morning came and went Tom thought about doing just that – consuming the last of his food and water in a final feast, saying a Hail Mary and an Our Father and sliding into the water. He thought he might float for a while and then dive below the surface and take in a lung full of water and that would be it, the end.

Around mid-afternoon Tom's attitude began to change. No matter what there's always a chance, a part of his brain kept telling him. Don't give up. Fight until your last breath. You aren't a quitter, don't go out that way.

Tom thought about praying. His days of being a believing Catholic were long over. As a child, he went to Catholic school and his father took him to Mass once a month or so, but by the age of 12 or 13 Tom simply drifted away from anything to do with religion. Science, particularly marine science, became his passion and his faith. God didn't seem to fit this equation – for Tom the very idea of God seemed an antiquated and almost primitive notion, at least the God he was taught about in Catholic school.

But given his dire circumstances a prayer seemed to be in order.

"God, the Universe, whatever you are, I need a little help. I really don't want to die out here. If I've blown it with you, I'm sorry. Thanks."

What a stupid prayer, Tom thought as he crossed himself. If God is out there he probably wants nothing to do with me.

He just lay there on the raft. He heard nothing all afternoon. There were no dolphins swimming by or fish jumping. He did see a couple of contrails in the sky; planes headed both east and west. As evening fell, Tom sat up on his fiberglass raft.

"I can't go out without a fight," Tom said aloud. "If I die, then I'll die doing my best to stay alive."

His internal battle was over, at least for the moment. But what the hell could he do? The only strategy that made sense to Tom was to do everything he could to stay alive for as long as possible. That meant conserving food, water and energy. It also meant avoiding depression and thinking positively, no matter how bleak things became.

Was it possible that a ship could happen by? He was not interested in lying to himself, he knew that he was well away from the major shipping lanes, but still this was the ocean. Ships travelled across the Pacific – hundreds if not thousands of them at any given time. Who knows what set of circumstances might bring a vessel near his position. Then the obvious occurred to him – what about another sailboat? His course wasn't a straight line from San Francisco to Hawaii, he deliberately chose to avoid as much traffic as possible, but might another sailor have the same idea?

Yes, that's it, Tom said silently to himself. The odds were fairly decent, maybe not great, but fairly decent that another sailboat could come within a few miles of his position. That could happen.

Tom reached into his red emergency pack and pulled out the flare gun. He loaded a shell into the gun and checked it. The gun appeared to be in working order. He tucked it back into the pack and tied it down with a strap.

He rehearsed in his mind exactly what he would do when he saw another boat. He would not be quick to pull the trigger on the flare gun; rather he would take a deep breath and try his best to determine the course and speed of the boat. If he could see that the boat was moving closer to him, he would wait to fire. Also, if it was near nightfall he would wait until the sky was darker before firing. How far away could his flare be seen? Several miles to be sure, but the boat might have to be traveling in his direction for anyone onboard to notice it. Would they be close enough to hear the flare explode? There were a number of uncertainties, but one thing was very clear – he only had three flares. He might have to decide to use them all at once, one after another, to get the attention of a boat or ship, or he might have to choose to hold his fire and wait for another opportunity.

His focus, his mission, was now set. Every moment he was awake, day and night, needed to be spent doing only two things

– sustaining himself physically and mentally and scanning the horizon for boats and ships. He vowed to do these things for as long as he could.

If his efforts were in vain then so be it. At least he would die knowing that he did everything he could to try and get back to his children. That might be the only solace he would have before he became fish food, but it was the best he could do.

◊   ◊   ◊

For the next four days, Tom settled into a routine. He watched the horizon for what he thought was an hour – his internal clock had always been pretty accurate – and then he closed his eyes and rested for about fifteen minutes. He repeated this process for the entire day and well into the night. When it was about midnight Tom allowed himself to sleep, willing his brain to wake him as close to dawn as was possible.

He was down to a few sips of water per day and a half of an energy bar. Also, he now slept with the emergency pack strapped across his chest and sitting by his left side. That system worked well enough; the only way he was going to lose the pack was if he went into the water with it.

By his calculations he had about ten days left. The food and water would run out in seven days and he figured that he could last three or four more days after that. If he survived for the entire time that would mean that he would have floated on the fiberglass raft for a little more than two weeks.

His spirits were up, or at least as up as they could be. He very diligently scanned the horizon, spinning around every few minutes or so thereby taking in a 360 degree view. All he saw was water and the occasional pod of dolphins. As he scanned the water, he thought about a lot of things.

Right below him was enough food and water to sustain him almost indefinitely. He could see the occasional fish swim by when he gazed down, but how was he supposed to catch them? When the debris field was still around he had looked for anything he could use as a pole and a hook or even a net, something, anything, to catch fish. He toyed with the idea of simply jumping in the water and trying to catch fish with his bare hands. That was a pointless effort, he quickly concluded. Not only would he be unable to catch any fish, he would exhaust himself in short order.

His mind drifted back to his children, to Syd and to the life he left behind. Good memories, troubling ones – they all jumbled together, coming at him in no particular order. At night he seemed to dream less and less.

His skin was getting burned and blistered. The sunscreen and aloe vera gel he found in the emergency pack was running low. He was thirsty and hungry constantly now – he almost could not remember what it was like to have a full belly or not to ache for water. But he kept his vigil, focusing as best he could on looking for any sign of human life on the water.

The sea had been calm, almost eerily so, ever since the explosion. On the evening of the sixth day after he was cast adrift, the weather began to change. Tom could see clouds approaching from the west, the typical direction storms moved over these waters. He was so accustomed to floating in tranquility that at times he almost forgot that the ocean was not normally this peaceful.

As the sun set the rain began. Then the once calm sea began to stir. By the time late evening arrived, Tom was hanging on for dear life as six foot swells tossed him and his fiberglass life raft around like ice in a blender.

Chapter Eighteen

The chunk of fiberglass Tom was holding on to for dear life had jagged edges. Sydney's hull had been ripped apart by the force of the explosion, and it did not tear neatly. These open edges now provided Tom with something he desperately needed, a place to hold on to.

His raft was a bit longer than his length, so he could put his hands into the side of the fiberglass and get and maintain a decent grip, but his feet were free to flop around. A strap was wrapped as tightly as possible around him securing the emergency pack to his side. He reminded himself that the emergency pack was buoyant – it might even be buoyant enough to act as a life preserver if he and the raft became separated.

But then again, if he and the raft became separated… that would be it.

As the storm raged on, the waves grew in frequency and size. Tom's headgear flew off in the wind. He had absolutely no control over where the raft went – he was riding a cork bobbing in a Jacuzzi on overdrive. The water crashed into him constantly, pounding his back and his face and forcing him to swallow seawater. This made him sick to his stomach so he began to retch with dry heaves. He knew this would only further dehydrate him, but there was nothing he could do to calm his stomach.

It was the wind and not a wave that turned his raft over the first time. Riding the crest of a swell, Tom could feel the wind literally pick him up and flip him over. Now he was hanging on to the fiberglass from the bottom side, underwater. His first thought at that moment was, it's over. I'm done for. Then instinct took over.

His head popped up above the waves and he took in a gulp of air. He still had a firm grip on the raft. But how was he going to crawl back up on top? Fortunately, the same forces that toppled him over now helped him get back up. As he tried his best to slide his right leg on top of the raft, a wave and a gust of wind pushed him in the same direction. Tom was lifted on top and hung on before he slid off the other side. The emergency pack also helped him – it made him totally buoyant.

He lay there on the raft for a while taking the battering and wondering if he could right himself again if he had to. He wasn't sure. He wanted to reach into his pack and take a sip of water, even a small amount might keep his stomach from cramping over and over again, but he dare not. In order to access the pack he would have to loosen the strap and if he lost the pack... again he would be doomed.

After a couple of hours of intense wind, rain and waves, Tom thought that the storm might be letting up a bit. How long would it be before dawn? Tom wondered. He thought it had to be three or four a.m., but there was no way to be sure. Even though he was in tropical waters, Tom was freezing. The combination of wind and wet on his bare skin was chilling him to the bone. When the sun came up he knew that he would go from being a Popsicle to a pizza in the microwave, but he preferred to roast rather than freeze.

The lull didn't last long, maybe half an hour. Then the sea came roaring back to life. The waves were higher and wind more fierce than it was before. After being slammed around by seven foot crests, he was flipped over once more. As he did the last time, Tom let the emergency pack bring him back up to the surface. Then the unthinkable happened.

He lost his grip on the raft.

Tom felt it slip away. He reached out for it, but when he did the raft was gone. The emergency pack was floating on his right side keeping his head above the water, but he was being battered by the waves every second. He could barely breathe. He couldn't think anymore, so he stopped struggling.

He put his right hand over the buckle that held the pack against his chest. All he had to do was unhook the buckle and it would be over. He would be forced under by the power of the waves and maybe he would feel some pain for a second or two, but that would be it.

Just as his hand was about to open the buckle, the raft him square in the head. It hurt like hell, jolting him back to life. He reached up and grabbed the side of the raft. The pack and the waves again acted in unison and almost gently set him back on top of the fiberglass.

"My God!" Tom screamed. Then he screamed again, "Enough!"

The sea did not listen to his pleas. It continued to roar for another hour or so, but then as the first rays of light began peaking over the eastern horizon the storm began to abate. Slowly at first, but then it quit almost at once.

Never before had Tom felt anything as good as the sun shining on his face and the taste of the fresh water that he now poured down his throat. He was fully aware that he was drinking three or four days' supply of water all in one big gulp, but he did not care.

For the entire day, Tom didn't do anything but lay on the raft and sleep. His brain needed some time to recover before he considered what he would do next.

Chapter Nineteen

"Yes, so what I really need to ask you is -."

"Can you hold please?" the woman on the line said.

"I have been... we were just talking... if I must, but -."

"Thank you. I'm the only one here at the moment. I'll be right back with you," the female voice reassured.

Syd was talking with the Hawaii office of the Coast Guard. She had expected to hear from Tom two or three days ago. While he had told her that there was no need to panic if he didn't check in "on-time", Sydney was terribly worried about him and had been since the moment he left San Francisco. She had not told the kids that she hadn't heard from their dad, there was no need to do that yet.

After the most maddening two minutes of her life, the woman came back on the line. "Sorry to put you on hold, I'm just a bit -."

"I need you to check on the status of my husband, Tom Campbell. His is sailing solo from San Francisco to Hawaii. He told me that he would be within radio range by now and I have not heard from him. I'm worried that something may have happened to him."

"Ma'am," the woman said, letting out a heavy sigh. "Do you know much about sailing?"

"Less than nothing. Why? What does it matter?" Syd was on the verge of losing her cool.

"Sailing is an imprecise way to move across the Pacific. Your husband is an experienced sailor I assume?"

"Yes he is."

"Then I'm sure he told you that things happen on long sail journeys. Over the past month, we have experienced some unusually calm weather in the northern and central Pacific – little or no winds for days at a time. Your husband probably just let his boat drift, went for a swim and enjoyed the incredible serenity of a glassy calm ocean. That's most likely the reason for his delay in reaching radio range."

"Yes, he told me things like that could happen. But I need you to check on him that's all I'm asking."

"How can we 'check on him'? Does he have a satellite phone? There is no radio or cell service in the middle of the Pacific."

"I wanted him to take a satellite phone, but he refused."

"Your husband probably does not want to be disturbed. That's not an unusual request from a -."

"Can't you send a ship or a plane to check on him? I see searches on TV going on all the time for people who are missing at sea."

"Your husband is not 'missing', ma'am. That's what I'm trying to tell you."

"How much would it cost to send a plane out to look for him? I'll pay the expense for you folks to do that, just tell me who to call and how much it is," Sydney said.

"It doesn't work like that ma'am, I'm sorry -."

"My name is Sydney, or Dr. Campbell, not ma'am."

The Coast Guard officer, Sydney was talking with the duty officer on station, took a deep breath. She knew from experience that people panicked when solo sailors were even a few days overdue.

"Dr. Campbell, we cannot send air resources to search for a sailboat that is not really overdue. Even if you had tens of thousands of dollars to pay for such a search, it would likely prove fruitless. The Pacific is a huge body of water. Your husband is a thousand miles away from any land. Finding one sailboat in the middle of the ocean is like, to use an old but appropriate cliché, trying to find a needle in a haystack."

"So there is nothing you can do?"

"I have noted that your husband is overdue. Before I put you on hold you gave me all the particulars; the boat's size and name, his planned course, his date of departure, all that. You also gave me your email and phone info. If you don't hear from him in a week or so, please call us back. I will alert this station that if he radios here for any reason, he should contact you immediately."

"There has to be something else I can do. We have two kids."

"You can worry less, that's what you can do. Ninety nine percent of the time there is nothing to be concerned about in these situations. I advise you against setting off any alarm bells with family and friends. Just give him a few more days and everything will be fine."

"Thanks. I'll try and take your advice. Please call me if you learn anything new."

"That's a guarantee. Goodbye, Mrs. Campbell."

"Goodbye."

Syd set her cell phone down and gazed out her window. Her home office looked out over the Bay, although it was few miles distant. She could see sailboats making their way through choppy seas. The winds had picked up in San Francisco over the past couple of days. She hoped Tom was enjoying these same conditions.

She picked her cell phone back up and dialed another number. It was Saturday afternoon, so she thought she might catch him at home.

"Hello," the man said.

"Gabriel, its Syd. Sorry to intrude on your weekend. Got a minute?"

"Syd... Yeah sure. Give me a second." Sydney could hear Gabriel talking to one of his daughters. "Yeah, Syd. How are you?"

"I'm fine. Listen, before we talk... I know I should have spoken with you more over the past year. We will always be family. I just thought it was awkward, you know, even though -."

"Syd, it's me you're talking to. Tom is my brother; you're the mother of his kids. Those two things will never change. What's on your mind?"

"Have you heard from Tom?"

"Nada. He wasn't planning on calling me until he arrived in Hawaii. Why? Is there a problem?"

"He was supposed to be in radio range by now. I've not heard from him."

"How many days is he overdue to call you?"

"Three or so," Syd said sheepishly, expecting that Gabriel was about to give her the same lecture as the Coast Guard officer did moments ago.

"I wish to hell that he'd have listened to me. Sailing all that way by himself... that was not his best idea."

"You're worried?" Syd asked.

"Been worried. Did you call the Coast Guard?"

"Just did. They said there is nothing they can do and that the winds have been weak over the past few days. They said to call them back in a while if I haven't heard from him."

"Yea, I'd expect them to say that. Sydney, you made the right call not letting Jonas go with Tom. I just thought you should know that."

"My son hates me for the moment, but what if... I can't imagine anything worse than to have both of them lost out there."

"Tom will be alright. Radios break down, ya know. He might be right on time and you'd still never hear from him until he made Honolulu."

"He has a cell phone," Syd said.

"Then he should be in cell range soon. My brother is one tough son of a bitch. You know that, right? He knows what he's doing on a sailboat. Let's try and not let our fears get the worst of us."

"Thanks, Gabriel. It's nice to know that you don't hate me."

"Why would I hate you? You're my sister for God's sake. Just because you and Tom split up doesn't mean that you stopped being my sister."

"I still love him, you know. Very much," Syd said. Her voice was now wavering as if she was about to cry.

"Take it easy, Syd. Everything will be alright. Call me any time of the day or night if you hear anything or if you just need to talk."

"Thanks, Gabriel."

Gabriel had been thinking a lot about Tom over the past couple of days. The big trial he was gearing up for was cancelled at the eleventh hour when the parties settled. Unfortunately, the settlement came a day after Tom left port. Gabriel had thought about radioing Tom or even trying his cell phone and asking him if he'd be willing to come back to San Francisco and pick him up, but he didn't want to disturb him. He figured that Tom was all set to do the trip solo, so why bother him and change his plans at the last moment?

Now Gabriel was really worried. What if Tom was in trouble? He knew that being three or four or even seven days late was no reason to panic, but his mind was filled with all sorts of bad thoughts. Tom had never had his appendix taken out. What if it ruptured? What if Tom had slipped and fallen and hurt his head? What if…

Stop it Gabriel, he chided himself, Tom is okay. He'll call Syd tomorrow or the next day and all will be well. I'm worried about nothing.

Chapter Twenty

How many days had passed since the storm hit? Two? Three? It couldn't be more than three, Tom was confident of that. While the storm had passed, the glassy seas were gone. There was a steady five knot breeze now, at least during the day. Tom was grateful for the light wind because the wind cooled him down, at least to a small degree.

Tom looked at his water bottle and gently shook it. There was only one tiny swig left. Once he consumed it that was it. The food was gone too. He ate the last bite of his final energy bar a few hours ago. Tom leaned back and swallowed the last of his water. He tipped the bottle up and tapped it on the bottom, hoping to shake free any lingering drop of liquid. He stuck his tongue inside and slurped up whatever moisture remained. Then he thought about tossing the bottle over the side, but for some reason he couldn't bring himself to do that so he tucked it neatly back in his emergency pack.

When he stored the bottle, he noticed the flare gun. He hadn't been too diligent about scanning for boats or ships over the past day or so. Mostly he'd stayed as still as possible. Now his mind had another thought – perhaps there was another use for the flare gun.

Three days from now, four at the most, Tom would breathe his last. He would die from a nasty combination of dehydration, starvation and exposure. Before he passed on he would lose his mind too. He would very likely hallucinate as his brain and body shut down from lack of sustenance and from baking hour after hour, day after day in the intense tropical sun.

Tom had used all of the aloe vera gel and sunscreen from the emergency pack. His skin was now almost charred, especially on his legs. Sun blisters were forming on his face and hands and they hurt like hell. As if the second degree burns weren't enough, his ribs were still on fire, more so the last couple of days.

So why not eat a flare? Tom asked himself. It wasn't the same as a bullet, but he had no doubt it would do the job. In his weakened condition a good knock on the head would probably end his life. Sure, it would hurt like hell, unimaginable pain, but only for a few seconds. Then it would be over. At least he could go out on his terms and not be a raving maniac when he died.

Over the years, Tom had known a few people who had committed suicide. While he was not judgmental, he felt nothing but sorrow for the victims and their families. He had vowed to himself that he would never go out like that. Tom believed that life was precious and should not be wasted for any reason.

That promise was an easy one to make from the cheap seats, but when you're lying on flotsam in the middle of the Pacific, burnt to a crisp with no food or water you begin to seriously contemplate ending your life in the least horrible way possible.

Stop it, Tom. Just stop it, he said silently to himself. No matter what I will fight to the end. I promised Jonas and Jessica I would do that. If nothing else, I'll keep my word.

Then off in the distance he saw something. It wasn't a boat or a ship, but it was moving. Then he saw it again. It was a whale, or rather a pod of whales all heading north. He couldn't see them clearly enough to identify the species, but they were large. He guessed they might be humpbacks on their way to Alaska to feed in the summer waters of the Artic Sea.

For a few minutes Tom lay there on his side and, shielding his eyes with his hands, watched as the whales swam by. He guessed that they must be close to a mile away from him. When they dove or simply swam out of range, Tom resumed his fetal type position on the raft.

He knew that the middle of the ocean, especially the Pacific Ocean, was like a desert. There was simply not enough food available here to sustain life, so the only creatures that were present were likely on their way to somewhere else. He had not seen even one shark since he'd been floating on the fiberglass.

At times, sometimes for an hour or more, he would look down at the water with his face almost in it. He couldn't put his face all the way in the water because if he did the salt water would cause his already sun blistered skin to burn like fire. When he looked down he saw the occasional fish swim by, all ocean going types. What appeared to be a rather large school of tuna had passed underneath him the day before the storm hit.

Why did this happen to me? That's the question Tom asked himself over and over again. He wondered if anyone would ever discover how Sydney blew up, or even that she did blow up. Yes, he had carved the simple inscription, "Tom Campbell was stranded here" onto the fiberglass, but would this chunk of fiberglass ever reach the shore? If it did, would anyone notice the words he spent hours carefully carving into the gel coat with the utility knife from the emergency pack?

The truth was he was going to die out here alone and there would likely be not a shred of evidence as to how or why. By now whatever was left of the debris field had sunk or was so scattered that no one would recognize it as the possible remains of a sailboat.

Over and over he thought about the same things. Why hadn't Stem to Stern been more diligent? A leaky propane tank or gas line should have been fairly easy to spot or, at a minimum, if the tanks were old or the lines were in poor condition the outfitter should have noticed this and replaced them.

He'd left his EPIRB hanging in the galley. He wanted to know exactly where it was in case Sydney went down. Now he understood why it was strongly recommended that sailors on solo voyages wear their EPIRB night and day because you never know. With the EPIRB activated, it would have sent out a signal that amounted to an SOS, a satellite monitored indicator of his GPS position. EPIRBs were noticed by the Coast Guard and, especially since he was mid-Pacific, an EPIRB signal from this location would have triggered a rescue operation.

He had a state of the art life raft at the ready too, carefully stored on deck. He'd spent nearly five grand on the thing. It even had a portable VHS radio with a 100 hour battery life.

What good did these items do him now? None. He had not prepared for an explosion. How do you prepare for an explosion on a sailboat anyway? The only thing you can do is be sure that....

I've got to stop doing this, Tom said to himself. I made a big mistake, not checking the propane tanks and gas lines, and a minor mistake, not wearing my EPIRB at all times. In general, I have always been a very careful sailor, never doing anything stupid.

Until now. It only takes once, Tom reminded himself.

It was sunset. How many more sunsets will I see? Tom asked himself. Knowing that he might not get many more chances, he lay there facing west. The wind died down as the sun slid into the water. He'd always wanted to see a green flash – a rare event that occurs only near the equator when the sun sets into the water. As the sun disappears, a green flash lights up the horizon.

But when the sun set there was no green flash. Better cross that off my list, Tom thought. Better cross everything off my list. Life will soon be over.

He didn't move at all as the night fell. He was gearing up for the switch from being too hot too being too cold. He knew the best thing he could do was sleep, so he did.

Chapter Twenty One

Time had no meaning now. It was either daylight or nighttime that was all he knew. Tom was either too hot or too cold. Any degree of physical comfort was only a memory. He tried to think about how long it had been since he had consumed water or food, but he had no idea. What he was sure of is that he would be breathing his last very soon. He wondered how he had survived this long.

His stomach was in a perpetual state of cramps. Every few seconds his gut reminded him that it was empty with painful contractions. He was almost used to this torture now, as if for his entire life he had been starving and dying of thirst. His lips were blistered and his mouth felt like it was made of sandpaper.

Sometime back – was it a week, day or an hour ago? – Tom tried to drink seawater. Not only did he feel as if he had ignited his mouth and lips, the minute the salt water hit his stomach he wretched with dry heaves. He could not stop vomiting for minutes. From then on he only used sea water as a cooling agent, but even that was now hard to do because the salt water burned his roasted flesh.

He thought, dreamed and regularly hallucinated. Tom saw his father walking on the water towards him, but when his dad reached the fiberglass raft he vanished like a soap bubble popping in the air. At times, Tom was sure that Sydney was on the raft with him. He had conversations with her. She reassured him that Jonas and Jessica would be alright that she would look after them and they would thrive and become healthy and happy adults. Once or twice Tom even felt Syd's arm around him, the way she would hold him when they spooned after making love. Yet somehow Tom knew that she wasn't real. He wanted to be with Syd, but he was horrified by the thought that she was out here with him. When her ghost vanished he was sad, but part of him was also relieved.

From time to time Tom thought about the flare gun. But despite the agony, the minute by minute excruciating hell he was enduring, he chose not to end his life literally in a flash. The instant escape of suicide was a temptation, but the thought of his children somehow learning that he had killed himself was simply too devastating to contemplate.

As the sun was setting, Tom thought he heard something. He could not be sure if anything he saw or felt was real, but he swore that he heard the sound of a boat or something floating near his raft. He looked up but saw nothing other than a disturbance in the water a few yards away. He assumed that it was a school of fish or a dolphin pod. He was too far away from land for a bird to be nearby. He thought that he probably imagined the whole episode.

When Tom woke up, the sun was rising in the east. He could barely move his head; much less his arms or legs. Breathing was difficult. He was facing west, but now he used his last bit of energy to look to the east. The sun was peaking over the horizon.

'It's so beautiful," Tom mumbled. He could barely speak because his mouth was dry, cracked and burned like fire.

Something told him it was time. He could barely see now, his vision was blurry at best. His stomach had stopped cramping as if to say, what for? There was simply no point in going on any longer.

Summoning all the strength he had left, which wasn't much, Tom inched his way down the fiberglass. The makeshift raft had been his home now for nineteen days, although he didn't know exactly how long it had been. Now he was saying goodbye to the raft, goodbye to the world.

When his foot hit the water it burned from the salt, which energized his brain just enough to make him a bit more consciously aware. He was expecting this. Tom hoped that the pain would be so intense when he slipped into the Pacific that he would pass out and just drift down into the depths.

When he managed to get his entire body in the water, he felt for an instant like he was being dipped in acid. He screamed in pain. Suddenly he was aware of where he was and what he was doing. Part of him wanted to try and climb back on the raft. There was still life left in him! But he just lay there on his back looking up at the bright blue sky.

Then Tom felt something underneath him. He assumed it was a pelagic fish or maybe a shark that had been trailing him waiting for an inevitable meal. Tom was certain that he was hallucinating. He told himself that he wasn't looking up at the sky and the clouds, he was drifting into the deep. He'd probably breathed in a lungful of seawater and was sinking. These were no doubt his last conscious thoughts...

But Tom could not shake the sensation that something was propping him up. He wasn't floating and now... it seemed impossible... he was moving. Then he felt water falling all over him as if it was raining. He reached down with his hands and felt rubbery flesh. What was happening?

Think Tom, think! he urged himself. What if this wasn't a hallucination? What if this was real?

Tom closed his eyes and opened them again. He managed to lean back on his elbows and sit up a bit. He was indeed riding on something, a large creature that was dark grey in color. He saw lighter spots on the creature's back...

"My God!" Tom screamed, but it came out as a squeak. "I'm riding on a sperm whale!"

This had to be a hallucination; he must surely be dead or dying floating on the surface or slipping into the depths. But part of his brain was desperately trying to convince him that this creature, a whale, was taking him somewhere. The whale must have surfaced underneath him when he slipped into the water and balanced him on his back. The whale was moving slowly in a specific direction. Where was he going? Tom wondered.

The amazing experience of being picked up and carried by a whale revitalized Tom, at least to the small degree that was possible given his proximity to death from exposure. His brain began to work again, at least minimally. He decided to accept the possibility that he wasn't dreaming this, that he was actually being taken for a ride on the back of a ...

No, it couldn't be, Tom thought. It simply wasn't possible. Tom managed to turn around enough to see the whale's giant fluke as it emerged from the water.

There was a piece missing from the whale's tail, where obviously a shark or an orca had taken a bite out of it many...

"Henry!" Tom yelled. This time he managed more than a squeak. "It can't be! Henry! Is it really you?!"

As if he heard him and wanted to respond, Henry sent a shower of seawater out through his blow hole drenching Tom.

For whatever reason, Tom decided to go with this version of reality. If he was imagining Henry picking him and carrying him away then what a beautiful dream! If he was dying or dead he wanted to go out this way, on the back of his beloved Henry. For a few moments, Tom did nothing more than sit there and ride as Henry moved north, or at least Tom imagined that he was moving north.

All of a sudden Henry stopped swimming. The whale did not try and shake Tom off or dive under the surface; he just floated there as if he was waiting for Tom to do something or for something else to happen.

Still in the euphoria of the moment, when Henry stopped moving Tom's body and brain reminded him that he was dying, fast. The initial surge of energy he felt was now gone. He wasn't sure what he would do next, but when Tom looked to his left he saw them.

Two of the red emergency packs from Sydney were floating right next to him and Henry! Tom again rubbed his eyes and opened and closed them. The packs were still there!

Acting on instinct, Tom slid off of Henry's back and into the water. He ignored the pain and reached for the packs. In a second he opened the first pack, grabbed a bottle of water and slugged it down. He reached inside for an energy bar and grabbed that and ate it in two bites. There was aloe vera lotion in here too and aspirin and...

Then Henry disappeared. Tom was floating using the backpacks as life preservers, but for a second or two he was once again terrified and confused. He was certain now that he was not imagining this because he could feel the water and food go down his throat. The pain from his skin burning in the salt water was intensifying as his senses were being revitalized.

Did Henry just take him to the emergency packs and drop him off? Where did he go? Was he...

Then Henry did what he had done before, he rose directly under Tom and floated to the surface. Now Tom was on Henry's back, nearer this time to the whale's small hump, and he had two emergency packs of supplies at his disposal. The whale did not move, as if he knew that Tom needed time to use the materials in the backpacks to bring him back to life.

Chapter Twenty Two

When the light from above was most intense and the water was very warm, Henry and some of his male sperm whale cousins knew that it was time to swim west toward the small areas of land that rose out of the sea. The whales did this once a year, as sperm whales had done for countless generations.

As Henry and two of his bull sperm whale cousins swam west, they were thinking about the food that was waiting for them at their destination – plentiful squid and octopus and demersal fish. They would not eat as much as normal on their journey. The ocean between California and Hawaii was largely barren, although the whales knew that if they dove deep enough they could probably find some food. But the long trek was worth it because the waters off of Hawaii teemed with life when the light from above was most intense.

Making their way west, the whales noticed familiar sights and sounds. At certain points of their long swim they saw many of the objects that floated on top of the water. The whales knew that the small creatures that walked on land were in these floating objects. One of the bulls swimming with Henry was very afraid of these floating objects and sent out the coda, "Predator, predator, predator" whenever one appeared. Henry and the other bulls were not as afraid, but they were wary.

The memory of how his mother died was very vivid in Henry's mind. But along with that horrible memory was also the idea that the small land creatures who floated on the objects that moved on top of the water did not intend to harm him or his mother. His memory was that these land creatures tried to help him. Especially the land creature he met when he swam onto the sand in panic.

Henry thought about this land creature from time to time, especially when he encountered the smaller objects that floated on the water. When Henry got close to these smaller objects he saw many of the land creatures looking at him and making joyful noises. Every time Henry encountered land creatures in this way he listened for the sound of the special land creature he knew and trusted, but he never heard his sound.

Most of the objects that floated on the water were very large, much bigger than whales. Henry knew that these objects took no interest in whales, but he also sensed that they should be avoided. His mother had been killed by an object like this, whether the object intended to kill her or not. On this journey, the larger floating objects paid no attention to the whales. This was normal and the whales simply kept their distance from them.

About halfway to their tropical destination Henry's cousins chose to dive down in search of a meal. Two periods of light and darkness ago Henry had been able to feed, so he was not interested in diving at the moment. As the other bulls headed down, Henry continued on his journey west but at a slower pace. The bulls would catch up with him after they fed and then they would then continue moving at full speed.

He wasn't sure why, but Henry sensed something. It was almost imperceptible, but it was a strange sound. He thought it was a sound made by a land creature, but Henry was sure that none of the objects that floated on water were nearby. It was during the time when the light in the sky was absent. Naturally curious, Henry swam towards the sound to investigate.

The whale popped up near a very small object floating on the water. Many times before Henry had found small objects floating on the water, but this one was different. A land creature was on top of this object. He was making noises too. Not loud noises, but Henry could hear him. It seemed to Henry that the land creature was calling out to another land creature, but there were no more floating objects nearby.

Everything about this small floating object and the land creature on top of it was odd and interesting. Henry had never seen a land creature on such a small object so far from land. There was something about this land creature too, something different, yet something familiar. During that first night, Henry popped up numerous times around the small floating object and listened and watched. The land creature was not moving much and Henry sensed that the land creature was in distress, perhaps great distress.

The next day Henry decided to explore the sea around this small floating object. He wanted to see if perhaps more floating objects were in the area. He found some more floating objects, but they were even smaller than the one the land creature was floating on. He approached them and noted their position and then returned to the where the land creature was floating.

As the light disappeared in the west, Henry surfaced near the small floating object. The land creature was making sounds again and Henry got close so he could hear them. He did not know what the sounds meant, but he heard, "Jessica… Jonas… Sydney," over and over again. Henry was close to the land creature now and could see and hear him very clearly.

Just as the light was disappearing, Henry went back down. The land creature heard or saw him, or so he thought, but he could not be sure. After swimming a short distance away, Henry sat almost motionless in the intense moonlight. He'd heard a coda from his bull companions a short while ago. They had eaten their fill and would be rejoining him soon. Henry sent back the message, "I am here".

Henry replayed the sound he heard the land creature make. It was familiar to him, but he had to play it over in his mind many times before he was sure. When he was certain, Henry returned to the small object floating in the water and surfaced.

Getting as close as he could Henry again looked and listened. The land creature wasn't moving or making any noises. Was it who Henry thought it was? Then the land creature made a loud noise, a sound of "Ahh!!!!" which Henry immediately understood meant that the land creature was in great pain.

It was him! The land creature Henry trusted, the land creature that had helped him so long ago! Henry was sure it was the same land creature because they had the same voice. Henry knew that creatures all made unique sounds. That's how he could tell them apart.

Henry could sense that the land creature that he trusted was in danger. He had no way of knowing for sure, but Henry had the thought the land creature might not be out in the water by his own choice, something else might have happened to him. Henry thought back to the time when his mother was struck by the large floating object. Maybe something like this had happened to the land creature he trusted. Perhaps a large floating object had struck him and now he needed help.

More than anything else Henry felt joy at the prospect of seeing and hearing from this land creature again. As he hovered just under the surface of the land creature's very small floating object Henry replayed in his mind what happened to him so long ago and how this land creature had made sounds that comforted him and had somehow moved him from the sand back into the sea.

When the light came from the east, Henry saw the land creature slip into the ocean. He was sinking fast and Henry knew that the land creatures, like him, needed to breathe above the water, not below it. So Henry surfaced underneath the land creature he trusted and took him above the water.

Then Henry had an idea. He would take the land creature to the objects he found floating in the water near here. Maybe these objects could help the land creature.

All Henry wanted to do was help.

Chapter Twenty Three

T om busied himself with the tasks required to stay alive. Henry was moving slowly to the southeast, not fast enough to jostle Tom from his back.

After drinking more water and eating two energy bars, Tom thought it might be safe to swallow three aspirin tablets. It was definitely a risk. Tom did not like the idea of his stomach revolting and cramping and puking, but he desperately wanted some relief from the agony.

Finding the sunscreen and aloe vera in the packs was like discovering a bag with a million dollars in it sitting by the side of the road. When Tom put the aloe vera lotion on his blistered skin, the soothing sensation was literally beyond words to describe.

Henry kept moving southeast. Tom kept working.

There were two emergency blankets, one in each of the back packs. Using a length of cord he removed from one of the backpacks, which he cut with a utility knife, Tom fashioned a makeshift cape. The blanket was bright silver. As a bonus, he thought that it might reflect the sunlight enough to flash in the eyes of a passing search plane. He tied the cape around his neck. The blanket covered his back completely with room to spare.

Tom took the second blanket and cut it up, creating a two foot long head scarf. He punched holes in his headgear so he could secure it. Then he weaved more cord through the holes and tied it around his forehead.

As he was doing this, Tom began to feel less pain. The aspirin was kicking in. While what he really needed was a hospital bed and an IV drip of morphine, he was very grateful for the aspirin.

Oh, and by the way, Tom thought to himself, I'm riding on the back of a fully mature, bull sperm whale in the middle of the Pacific Ocean.

To his surprise, Tom did not have to struggle to stay on Henry's back. Where he was perched it was almost flat. Somehow Henry was moving at just the right pace. It was kind of like riding on an enormous cow that had wet rubber skin.

Then Henry stopped. Tom thought it must be mid or late afternoon. They were miles and miles away from his fiberglass raft now. Henry did not dive, but Tom was almost deafened when the whale released a series of loud blasts directed to the deep. Henry was telling his whale buddies something, but what? Tom was still in tremendous pain, but the wonder and awe of what was happening to him was fast becoming the most powerful feeling he was experiencing.

Henry sent the coda, "Go on without me, go on without me." His bull calf cousins asked him to repeat the coda, which Henry did. Then Henry remained motionless in the water.

The whale could sense that the land creature he trusted was now experiencing joy and was no longer afraid. Henry had only one thought about what to do next. He would return the land creature he trusted to the place where the land creature had saved him. Henry thought that this place on the sand must be where the land creature wanted to go.

With a gentle but powerful kick of his fluke, Henry took off on a new course. He was still headed southeast, but now slightly more south than east. He moved faster now but not fast enough, Henry hoped, to cause the land creature distress.

Tom tied both of the emergency packs together into a bizarre whale saddle bag type configuration. Keeping his legs apart behind him for balance, Tom lay down on his stomach on the remnants of the second emergency blanket that he had placed between the two packs. While he did not fall asleep, for the first time in three weeks Tom was almost calm.

He had no idea where Henry was going or even if he would survive the day, but Tom wanted to rest so he could to be as fully present as possible for whatever happened next.

◊   ◊   ◊

"Yes, Mrs. Campbell. This is Lieutenant Watkins. We spoke a few days ago. We have not heard anything from your husband yet."

Sydney took a deep breath. Her patience had reached it limits. "Yes, I'm sure you would have called me if you'd heard anything. I need you to begin a search and rescue operation immediately."

"Yes ma'am. I understand your -."

"Commander Robinson… he's the officer in charge at your station, yes?" Syd asked, already knowing the answer to her question.

"Yes ma'am, he is," the Lieutenant acknowledged.

"Have you discussed this matter with him this morning?"

"No, I haven't but… It seems as if he is trying to reach me as we speak. May I ask you to hold for a minute or two?"

"Please. I'm not going anywhere, Lieutenant," Syd said.

Lieutenant Watkins put Sydney on hold. She knew that this was Commander Robinson's day off so if he was trying to find her something was indeed up.

"Sir," Watkins said as she punched in the correct line.

"Lieutenant, initiate a full scale search and rescue operation immediately for Thomas Campbell. Have you loaded SAROPS yet?"

"No sir," Watkins said. "Mr. Campbell is not sufficiently overdue. As you know, winds were unseasonably light in the area and we -."

"Initiate SAROPS, establish a search grid. Air resources and cutters, everything we've got."

"Yes sir. May I ask why we are taking these steps, sir? Protocol would say that -.""

"I have received two phone calls this morning, Lieutenant. One was from the Chairman of the House Oversight committee for the Coast Guard; the other was from the senior Senator from California. Do I really have to waste even one more second explaining this to you?"

"No sir. I'm on it."

"Full blown search. All resources deployed. Do I make myself clear Lieutenant?"

"Perfectly clear, yes sir."

"Good. I'll be in the station in an hour. I expect a full report when I arrive."

"Yes sir." After Watkins acknowledged the order, the Commander ended the call.

"Mrs. Campbell?" Watkins said as she reconnected to Syd's line.

"Right here, Lieutenant," Sydney said.

"A full scale search and rescue operation has been initiated for your husband. Until further notice, I'll be handling the operation personally. You can contact me at any hour of the day or night and receive progress reports."

"Thank you, Lieutenant," Sydney said.

"We will do everything we can to find and retrieve your husband as quickly as possible."

When Sydney hung up the phone in her home office, she saw Jonas standing behind her. He had heard every word she said to the Coast Guard.

"You were going to tell me about this when, Mom?" Jonas said.

"Right after I made this call. Sit down, Jonas."

"So this is why all those people were calling you last night. The lady from the Senator's office?"

"Yes, son."

"Where's Dad?" Jonas asked.

"He's overdue. I… the Coast Guard is sending out people to look for him. That's what I've been arranging."

"I should be with him. You wouldn't let me go and now he's out there all by himself with no one to help him."

"Jonas, I… look, the truth is I'm the one who is probably panicking. He's not that overdue, barely a week. I'm worried, I need to do -."

"He wouldn't be out there right now if you hadn't divorced him."

Sydney didn't say another word. She looked away from her son and started to cry. Jonas didn't try and comfort his mother; he turned and left the room.

Chapter Twenty Four

When night fell, Henry stopped and floated in the water. Tom was feeling better, but he was by no means in anything close to good shape. His ribs were on fire and his skin, while vastly improved by the aloe vera treatments, was blistered and bleeding. He had eaten five of his fifteen energy bars in one day and drank nearly half of his water. Now he was more exhausted than he had ever been before in his life. All he wanted to do was sleep.

"Can you hear me, Henry?" Tom said, almost shouting at the whale. "How did you find me out here? Where are you...?" Tom stopped talking, took a deep breath and said simply, "Thank you, my friend."

Henry had no idea what the sounds coming from the land creature he trusted meant, but he remembered the tone, the inflexion of the land creature's voice. It was the same tone the land creature used when he helped Henry on the beach. Henry had come to believe that this tone meant, "You are safe, you are safe". So Henry clicked back, at a very restrained decibel level, "You are safe, you are safe".

Tom couldn't believe what was happening. He and Henry were communicating, at least as much as that was possible! He knew better than to assume that a whale thought like a human did, but Tom was sure that a core message of gratitude getting through; both gratitude and friendship, a connection.

There was also no doubt in Tom's mind that Henry recognized him and knew that he was the same man who helped save him on the beach all those years ago. Now more rested and rejuvenated, Tom's brain was working again. Over the past couple of hours he tried to recall everything he knew about sperm whales. At one point in his life Tom Campbell was a walking sperm whale encyclopedia, but over the years some of that information had dissipated or had been replaced with more pressing concerns.

But Tom was able to focus on a few key facts. Sperm whales were highly intelligent creatures. Was this whale capable of recognizing him after two decades? From visual appearance alone almost certainly not. Humans often can't recognize other humans after such long periods, particularly if they had only limited contact with the other person in the past. But whales were auditory creatures. They sensed the world primarily through sound.

"You recognized my voice, is that it?" Tom said as he gently stroked the whale. "Okay, I can buy that. But what led you to me out here? How is that -."

Interrupting himself, Tom thought about his question again. Why would a sperm whale be in the middle of the Pacific Ocean mid-summer? He might be here if he was headed to the Hawaiian Islands to feed. This theory made sense. As far as Tom knew, his position could be just right for a whale to run into him if he was traveling from Central California waters westward.

"I guess I'll just have to leave the rest up to my imagination..." More thoughts and ideas were invading Tom's brain, but he knew that he had to turn them off.

"Alright big guy, I need to go to sleep. I'd rather not wake up floating in the ocean holding on to my emergency packs for dear life. You won't leave me out here, will ya?"

Henry didn't respond this time, but he remained stationary.

"I wonder how much you know," Tom asked aloud. "Anyway my friend, try not to knock me off when you start moving. I'm passing out now."

Using his cape as a kind of blanket, Tom laid down on his stomach like he'd done when Henry was moving. Within seconds, he was asleep.

◊　　　◊　　　◊

"Report," Commander Robinson said as he sat down in his office chair. Lieutenant Watkins, two other officers and three NCOs were waiting to brief him.

"SAROPS analysis of Campbell's likely position resulted in a search grid of over a thousand square miles. We have deployed two C-130 aircraft to begin visual search patterns. A cutter is also moving to the general area to search the most promising SAROPS target area."

"How soon until the C-130s reach the grid and begin their search patterns?" Robinson asked.

"Within the hour, sir," an NCO answered.

"Tell me about Campbell," Robinson ordered.

"He's fifty years old, in excellent physical condition and an experienced sailor. His sailboat, Sydney, is a thirty foot Rawson sloop. According to the outfitter in San Francisco, the boat is in mint condition. I have the outfitter's report here. It was written the day before Campbell left San Francisco. Would you'd like to review it, sir?" Lieutenant Watkins asked.

"That won't be necessary," Robinson said. "A thirty foot boat, okay... communications on board?"

"Ship to shore radio, cell phone and an EPIRB," Watkins reported.

"I assume that we have checked all of the EPIRB frequencies and continue to monitor them?" Robinson asked.

"Twenty four seven, sir. Standard protocol," Watkins reported.

"How overdue is Campbell?" the Commander asked.

"Eight days plus, sir," another NCO answered.

"He's probably out there safe and sound just taking his bloody sweet time... Ah well. We live in the world we live in people. Campbell's ex-wife is a famous author with some serious ties to the Hill. We're being watched on this one, so let's shine. Find this guy soon and preferably in one piece, please. Dismissed."

◊　　◊　　◊

"Hi Gabe," Syd said as she opened her front door and let Gabriel Campbell in. "Where are your bags?"

"I'll stay at Tom's place, Syd. Easier for everyone that way. I assume that Harold's here?"

"He is, but he's not a problem. Harold only wants what's best for the kids and he sure as hell doesn't want their father to be lost at sea."

"Sure... Yes, Syd, for sure. I think I'll stay at Tom's though. Where's Jonas?"

"Upstairs."

"Does he know I'm coming?"

"Yes, I told him."

"I might take him over to Tom's place with me for a night or two if that's alright with you."

"I think it might do him some good. Jonas is very upset. He basically hates me and he's worried sick about Tom."

"Jess?" Gabriel asked.

"She's keeping everything in, as usual. I've talked to her about it, but she seems almost un-phased."

"How 'bout you?" Gabriel said as he leaned over and gave his sister-in-law a kiss on the cheek and a strong hug.

"I'm a wreck. The Coast Guard is finally out looking for him, thank God. But I feel like... I ... I mean, what if something bad happened?"

Syd teared up and Gabriel held her for a minute in the entryway. Then he kissed her on the cheek and went upstairs to find his nephew.

"Hey Jonas," Gabriel said as he knocked and went through Jonas' partially opened bedroom door.

"Uncle Gabe!" Jones said and rushed over to get a hug. "Thanks for coming."

"How ya doin'?" Gabriel asked.

"Where's my Dad?" Jonas asked.

"I'm sure he's alright. A lot can happen out there, not all of it totally terrible. Your mother is doing everything she can to help."

"I should be out there with him."

Gabriel sighed and squeezed his nephew's shoulder. "No son, I should be out there with him. Don't lay that weight on yourself."

"But Mom, she should -."

"Your mother loves you, Jonas. She needs you to be strong. Stop blaming her for things. That's not the way to handle this situation. Your dad would not want you making it harder for your mom right now."

"I guess... I -."

"Hungry?" Gabriel asked.

"Big time."

"Cheeseburger, fries and a shake?"

"Oh yeah. I've had way too much healthy food lately. Harold is a vegan, ya know. Mom is becoming one."

"Off we go then," Gabriel said. "Oh, and pack a bag. We're staying at your dad's house. Let me go say hi to Jess and we're outta here."

Chapter Twenty Five

It was raining again. Tom was in San Francisco casually strolling to work through the financial district. He looked up and got soaked. Tom walked another half a block and he was hit by another blast of water. He caught a little in his hand and tasted it. It was salt water. Since when…

Opening his eyes, Tom realized that he'd been dreaming. The rain was spray from Henry's blowhole. The whale wanted him to wake up, or maybe Henry was just checking to see if he was carrying a corpse.

Tom tried to sit up, but at first he couldn't move. The muscles in his back were severely cramped, so he stretched for a few seconds before he sat up. Then he took stock of his situation. No, it had not been a dream. He really was perched on the back of a giant whale. The emergency packs were still right in front of him. He had water! He was parched. Unlike yesterday, Tom used some judgment. He sipped the water, he didn't gulp it.

The aloe vera lotion treatments he'd applied yesterday helped, but he needed to do it again right now. He wondered if Henry would wait for him to do this before he started swimming. Maybe I just say something like, "Giddy up, Henry" when I want him to move. Tom laughed at his joke.

His brain was working today, nearly on all cylinders. As Tom applied the green lotion to his legs and then to his torso and back he realized that the burns on his skin were serious. Some of the burns were second degree or worse. Infection would become a problem soon. After putting on the aloe vera gel, Tom slathered on sunscreen. His ribs were also barking at him, but as far as he could tell they were not broken. He ate two energy bars and swallowed five aspirins.

From the position of the sun in the sky, Tom guessed it was less than an hour after sunrise. He was ready to move if Henry was. After a few moments of remaining still, Henry hit him with another blast of water from his blowhole.

"Okay, I get it. How do I tell you it's okay to start swimming? Let's see, what if ... whoa!!!"

The whale kicked his massive tail and they were off. Henry was moving a bit quicker today. How fast were they traveling? Tom had nothing to gauge this by other than feel. He knew that sperm whales could move as fast as twenty miles per hour on the surface for up to an hour, but Henry was not swimming that quickly.

"Henry is moving about the same speed I was going in Sydney," Tom said aloud. He knew this pace well, about seven or eight miles per hour.

As Tom sat there watching the ocean pass by he searched his memory for any recollection of a sperm whale doing anything like this before. Certainly Orcas have been trained to carry humans on their backs and dolphins and humans had been touching each other for millennia, but a sperm whale acting like this? It was unprecedented, it had to be.

"What if no one ever knows about this?" Tom said aloud. He realized that he was having a conversation with Henry, but he did not expect an answer. If by some miracle, and he was living a miracle at the moment so why not expect more to come, he got through this ordeal alive would anyone believe his story? What if

Henry sees a ship and just dumps me off? Would anyone in their right mind believe my tale? Tom knew that he wouldn't believe it unless he lived it.

"We've gotta make sure that doesn't happen, Henry," Tom said. This was something that had to be shared with the world. "Maybe the few idiots left on the planet who kill whales will be forced to stop doing it after they learn about you and me."

The whale encyclopedia in Tom's brain kicked in again. Over the centuries people slaughtered sperm whales by the hundreds of thousands, primarily for their spermaceti oil, from which they were given their common name. The oil is stored in their head and it's believed that the oil may offer the whale some protection from the stings of giant squid, one of their primary sources of food. Human beings no longer have any legitimate commercial use for spermaceti oil, but in the 19th century and earlier it was a prized economic resource.

In his mind Tom could see the pictures of the old whaling stations in America, Australia, Russia and Japan where sperm whales carcasses were brought in by the hundreds by whaling fleets. It was a nightmarish vision. Tom had always believed that whaling for any reason was morally wrong, with the possible exception of the small whale harvest taken by native peoples in the Artic.

"How could we slaughter such a magnificent creature?" Tom said aloud. "Have you forgiven us for being so cruel and stupid, Henry?" Tom laughed. Whales were very intelligent, but concepts like hate and love and forgiveness and unforgiveness were probably completely foreign to them. But then again…

Tom looked at Henry's skin. It was almost prune like, which was proving to be a huge advantage in riding the whale. Henry's skin was not exactly grip tape, but because of the whale's unique skin texture, massive girth and gentle traveling speed staying on top of Henry was surprisingly effortless. Every so often Henry would send out a blast of water from his S shaped blowhole. Tom had learned now to duck when he saw the water coming. Otherwise, the salt would sting his eyes.

I wonder what we'd look like from above? Tom asked himself silently. Satellite imagery from space could focus in on an object as small as a license plate. Tom imagined someone looking at a screen and seeing a man with a silver cape and a silver bandana riding on the back of a fifty ton sperm whale. What a visual!

"That's what we need my friend. That's really the only thing that will do. We need to make you a media sensation," Tom shouted at the whale. Laughing to himself, Tom remembered that Henry had already been a media sensation two decades ago.

The day went on and Tom tried his best to soak up every thought, every sight and every sound of the experience. He was at peace, almost incredibly so. He only got anxious when he thought about Jess and Jonas. Was the Coast Guard out looking for him yet? Knowing Sydney the way he did, Tom was sure that she hit the panic button sooner rather than later.

But Henry was rapidly taking him away from any reasonably defined search area. If they did send aircraft or even a ship out to look for him they would find nothing but empty ocean, or perhaps a small chunk of fiberglass with his name carved in it.

◇   ◇   ◇

Watkins knocked on Commander Robinson's door. She heard "Come" in response.

"No sightings yet from the C-130s, sir," the Lieutenant reported. "They have covered about half of the search grid."

"Will they finish the grid by nightfall?" Robinson asked.

"Probably not, but they'll cover 75% of it," Watkins answered.

"What about other commercial or private vessels in the area?"

"There is commercial traffic in the southeast quadrant of the grid. We have reached a few other private craft, also sailboats, who are entering the area now. They have been alerted to look for Sydney and they are sending out radio messages to Sydney every half an hour," Watkins reported.

"So, no response from Sydney... we can conclude that his radio is out," Robinson said.

"That's fair," Watkins agreed. "Campbell is experienced enough to not turn off his radio, regardless of his position from shore."

"Keep Mrs. Campbell informed," Robinson said.

"Aye aye, sir," Watkins said and then she turned and left.

◊   ◊   ◊

Behind him and to his port side, Tom could see the sun setting. When the sun was almost below the horizon, Henry stopped swimming. How far had they traveled today? Tom was trying to keep at least a rough calculation in his mind; maybe a hundred miles, or perhaps a bit less. Henry was still headed southeast. Where was he going? The whale seemed to have a specific destination in mind.

One thing Tom was sure of was that sooner or later Henry would cross major shipping lanes. The odds were pretty good that they would spot a ship, most likely a passing freighter. In his emergency packs were two flare guns. Tom had already loaded them.

Henry was "logging" again. Tom remembered earlier in the day that this was the term used to describe what a sperm whale did while he was resting. The whale was lying motionless with part of his head and back exposed to the surface while his tail was hanging down.

The moon was full tonight. Tom took out his water bottle and took another couple of sips as he watched the moonlight dance off of the water. Everything was incredibly still. At this moment, more than anything else Tom wished for a camera. No, he thought some more, a satellite phone and a camera.

Henry was breathing slowly and rhythmically. Clearly the whale knew exactly what he was doing. Part of what he was doing was keeping Tom Campbell alive, but he was also taking him somewhere, but where? The nearest point of land from here, at least as far as Tom could roughly calculate in his head, would be Central California near Santa Barbara or perhaps the islands in the channel directly off that coastline.

"Is that where you're going, my friend? To the nearest point of land?" Tom paused and took in the incredible seascape in front of him. "I hope I can hang on that long." How many days to get there? Ten? A couple more? Would Henry keep going in the same direction, or change course?

Like he had the night before, Tom laid out the remnants of the second emergency blanket on Henry's back in between his red packs and lay down. Once more, he quickly fell asleep.

Chapter Twenty Six

As light began to shine in the east Henry realized that he was very hungry. Normally he would consume as much as a ton of food daily. His energy level was low, so he had to eat soon. From experience, he knew that he could find enough food to satisfy his hunger in these waters if he went deep enough.

Henry wondered if the land creature he trusted was also hungry. He did not know for sure what the land creature ate, but he assumed that he must eat fish. Many of the objects that floated on top of the water collected fish. Sperm whales assumed that the land creatures gathered fish so they could eat them.

As he had done for the previous two days, Henry woke Tom up with a blast from his blowhole. Tom was expecting this and rose quickly, drank some water and applied his skin lotions. Henry continued to move on the same course he'd been on since he rescued Tom.

About half an hour into his swim, Henry stopped. Then the whale sent out the only coda he thought the land creature who he trusted knew, "You are safe, you are safe".

Tom didn't know what to think. Why was Henry stopping? What was he trying to tell him?

Henry repeated the coda, "You are safe, you are safe." Then Henry slipped under the surface.

"Holy crap!" Tom yelled as he grabbed ahold of his emergency packs, which were now his life preservers. Within seconds, Henry was gone.

Now Tom was floating in the middle of the Pacific with only his red packs standing between him and certain death. While he did not have to kick to stay afloat, Tom was well aware that his dangling legs made a tempting target for any passing shark.

"What do I do now?" Tom said. Was Henry gone for good? Did he save me only to just drop me off? He'd gone from relatively relaxed to scared out of his mind in a few moments. Tom took a deep breath and decided that the most likely reason Henry left him was to feed. Sperm whales ate every day when they could.

"He'll come back, he has to," Tom said aloud, encouraging himself.

Fifteen minutes passed, then thirty. The good news was Tom had not seen any evidence of sharks or any other fish, in his vicinity. The bad news was Henry was still gone. How long did it take for a sperm whale to -.

Tom's thoughts were interrupted by a blast from the deep. A pressure wave was rising up through the water. He could hear the blast, but he felt it more than heard it. Something was coming at him from below, something that was making a lot of noise.

"I'm going to die," Tom said. All he could do was hang on to the packs and wait for the giant mouth that was no doubt speeding towards him to swallow him whole. Tom closed his eyes when another blast of sound or pressure or whatever hit him from below.

Then he heard a strange sound, something like popcorn popping in a microwave bag. When his face was splashed by something, Tom was forced to open his eyes.

All around him were common flying fish, Parexocoetus brachypterus. There were dozens of them just lying on the surface. Were they dead? Tom soon learned that not all of them were when one of the fish a few feet away from him took off in a rush. But the others weren't moving.

Sashimi! Tom's brain told him. A feast is in front of you! Before he thought anymore about how or why the fish got here,

Tom pulled his utility knife out of the pack and reached for a fish. Leaning over a pack, Tom cut the head off of the fish and set the carcass on top of the pack that he was not balancing on. He did this for a dozen more fish when suddenly, all at once, the vast majority of the fish around him came to their senses and either flew away across the water or just slipped back into the sea.

After gathering five more fish that were clearly dead, Tom stopped and took stock of what he had – almost twenty fresh flying fish right in front of him ready to be eaten.

"Henry!" Tom yelled. It had to be Henry! As he busied himself with fileting his first fish, Tom thought about sperm whales and how they fed. Unlike humpbacks and dolphins and some other marine mammal species, sperm whales did not bubble fish - capture fish en masse by surrounding them with a stream of bubbles. But somewhere in his mind Tom recalled a scientist positing the theory that sperm whales used sonar blasts to stun fish and then eat them. As far as Tom knew this theory had never been proven, this behavior was not yet documented in the wild... until now.

The first bite of flying fish was pure heaven. Nothing had ever tasted so good! The fish satisfied both Tom's hunger and his thirst. He had gobbled down three more before his brain urged him to slow down.

A full belly resulted in a few minutes of very unpleasant cramping and then a violent defecation. Once that unpleasantness was over Tom felt better than he had since the Sydney exploded. His blistered skin was sore from exposure to salt water, but he had consumed five more aspirins and that eased the pain.

How long had it been since Henry left? At least two hours or maybe more. Tom looked around him. He was sitting in a field of chum! Surrounding him a neat little circle were a few dead flying fish, severed fish heads and guts plus the mess he'd made after he ate. Talk about ringing the dinner bell! Tom gently paddled away from the blood and guts. He didn't want to go too far, but floating in the middle of all of that was definitely not a good idea.

Another hour passed. Tom was getting worried again. He was sure that Henry had not abandoned him when he sent the flying fish his way, but what if that was just a parting gift? Here's some food, see ya later? That was certainly a possibility.

Tom began to think about what he could do with the resources he had. He thought it might be possible to climb on top of both packs – propping his head on one and his feet on the other with his butt in the middle. Would that offer any real protection from hungry predators approaching from below? It might. Also, the flare guns he had could be aimed at the open mouth of a shark. The noise and commotion caused by the blast might be enough to …

Then from beneath him Tom could feel the whale slowly rising to the surface. He scrambled to center himself on the whale's back a few feet in front of the hump. Luckily, he only lost a few of his fileted flying fish in the process. Dinner was secure.

"I've never been happier to see anyone in my life old boy!" Tom yelled at the whale. "I love you Henry!"

Henry didn't respond with a coda, he just floated there logging. After a few minutes, Henry spouted a huge blast from his blowhole. Tom was learning, he knew what this meant.

"Onward ho, my friend," Tom said, laughing. Henry began to swim at the same steady pace on the same course as before.

Chapter Twenty Seven

"You need to tell me that one more time, please. Slowly," Syd said. She was talking with Lieutenant Watkins, who had woken her up at three in the morning.

"A sailboat passing through the search area found some debris or possible debris. We don't know if it's from Mr. Campbell's boat or not. There isn't much; some rope, a bit of charred sail, a pair of shorts, one sock and a shirt."

"What do you want me to do?" Sydney asked.

"It's a longshot, but we need to ask you if you can identify any of this material as belonging to your husband…, ah... ex-husband."

"Do you have pictures?"

"Yes, jpeg files. Can I send them to the email address you provided me with earlier?"

"Yes, please send them now. I'll look at them and call you back as soon as possible."

"Thank you, Ms. Campbell."

Sydney looked at the clock and reconfirmed that it was indeed the middle of the night. Harold was fast asleep. Poor man, Syd thought. He has been so supportive of me and the kids, doing his best to give comfort in what had to be the most awkward and uncomfortable situation imaginable. She leaned over and gave him a kiss on the cheek. Harold stirred, but did not wake up.

After putting on her robe, Syd walked down the hall to her home office. She passed Jessica's room and peeked inside. Her daughter was asleep, but her headphones were on and Syd could hear music still playing through them. Her first instinct was to turn off the music and remove her headphones, but Syd decided against that. If Jessica liked to sleep that way then Syd decided it would be a mistake to intervene, especially tonight.

After turning on the light and sitting down at her desk, Syd switched on her laptop. Her heart was racing. Did she want to find that these objects belonged to Tom or not? Would that mean he was more likely to be dead or alive? More information is always better, Syd told herself in a clinical, positive self-talk tone. She wasn't at all sure if she believed that…

The first jpeg file was a photo of a short strand of rope and some sail. Nothing there, Syd said to herself. The next was a deck shoe. It was blue. A note on the file said the shoe was size eleven. That was Tom's size, but there were maybe half a billion other males on the planet who also wore a size eleven shoes. She tried to recall if Tom ever wore blue deck shoes. Searching her memories she simply couldn't recall the color of Tom's deck shoes, so she moved on to the next file.

Two pairs of shorts, one faded red the other khaki. Waist size thirty. Was Tom a thirty or a thirty two waist? Syd clearly remembered that he was a thirty two waist. However, since they split he had lost some weight. Enough to fit these shorts? Probably not, Syd concluded, but she could not be sure.

The last jpeg file was the shirt. It was a faded Los Angeles Dodgers tee shirt, size large. Syd's heart raced again. She zoomed in on the collar. There it was. The right side of the collar had been torn and re-sewn with black thread.

Sydney put her hand over her mouth and muffled a scream. Her hands were shaking and she was crying. She had never felt so frightened in her entire life.

Five years ago Syd had re-sewn that old tee shirt for Tom. He considered it to be his lucky charm. Whenever the Dodgers made the playoffs he wore the old rag, claiming they never lost a game when he wore it and sat a certain way in his favorite chair watching the ballgame.

Closing her eyes Syd could see Tom sitting in his old Lazy Boy recliner, the chair she hated so much, cheering for the Boys in Blue, as he called his favorite team. Then she remembered getting upset with him because he had not done this or that household chore or something else trivial that day that she wanted him to do. This made her cry even more.

Get it together, Syd, get it together. I've got to maintain here! I can't lose it, the kids need me, Tom needs me, Harold needs... Then she broke down again. It was an hour and three cups of coffee later before Sydney was composed enough to call Lieutenant Watkins back.

"Yes, Ms. Campbell," Watkins said, picking up the line.

"The Dodgers tee shirt belongs to Tom. I'm 100% sure of it. There is a black thread mend on the collar. I mended that shirt years ago."

"I need to ask you one more time. You're sure, no doubts."

"No doubts," Syd repeated. "What does this mean? Where is Tom?"

"It means that almost certainly his sailboat sank. We analyzed the piece of sail. It had been burned."

"Meaning what?" Syd asked.

"We can't be sure of course, but the most logical interpretation of the evidence suggests an onboard fire – a catastrophic on board fire."

"My God," Syd mumbled. All of the composure she had worked so hard to build now crumbled. Watkins could hear her crying and sniffling through the phone.

"Don't jump to the worst conclusions yet, Ms. Campbell. We reviewed the manifest provided by the boat's outfitter in San Francisco. There was a state of the art emergency life raft on board. Mr. Campbell could survive in that raft for days, weeks even with a little luck."

"I've been reading about sailboats...Looking at nothing else really for the past few days. Tom had an EPIRB, I'm sure of it. You have not received any signal from an EPIRB that might be him?"

"No, we haven't. That's not good news, but EPIRBs are powered by batteries. Batteries fail. Emergency radios fail. It would be wrong to conclude from your positive ID of this debris that Mr. Campbell is deceased. We don't know that and, in fact, now that we are nearly certain that his boat went down we will intensify the search."

"I thought you were already doing everything you can," Syd said.

"Sorry, I used the wrong term. We are adjusting our search pattern now based on where this debris was found. We use the most comprehensive and effective computer system on the planet, SAROPS or Search and Rescue Optimal Planning System. It takes into account literally all the information we gather and plots an optimal search grid. Finding and identifying this debris will allow us to search more effectively for Mr. Campbell. That's a positive development, Mrs. Campbell."

"You will call me the instant you learn anything new."

"Yes ma'am. I'll call you at least once every 24 hours, but not again in the middle of the night unless that's absolutely necessary."

"Thank you."

"Hang in there, Ms. Campbell. We're really just getting started and we're very good at what we do."

◊   ◊   ◊

Day three of Tom's whale ride adventure began exactly the same way the first two days started with a blowhole alarm waking him up shortly after dawn. Tom was feeling better now, much better. He knew that, to some degree, this improvement was superficial. He could be bleeding internally and parts of his skin, especially a black colored patch on his right thigh, were severely burned.

But he was riding on the back of a sperm whale. Because he had done this now for seventy two plus hours Tom was adjusting to the experience – what once seemed miraculous was now almost normal. He was ready, at least as ready as he could be, to respond to another dive by Henry. He worked it out in his mind and he was fairly certain that he could prop himself up above the water on his emergency packs. Sort of like a pool lounge chair, only I'm in the middle of the ocean! He laughed about it. I'll just lay back and wait for the sushi to pop up!

They were swimming along, still headed southeast. Tom's most important observation so far was that some type of disturbance was moving in from the west. He wondered what it would be like to ride out a storm on the back of a sperm whale. He guessed that it would take a might frothy ocean to bounce around a creature of this size.

Then he heard it. At first he couldn't be sure, but then he was positive. Propellers! A plane was closing in on his position. Wishing that he had a pair of sunglasses, Tom tried his best to identify the position of the plane in the sky from the sound. The best he could tell the plane was approaching him from the northeast. This meant looking directly into the morning sun.

Henry was un-phased by the plane or Tom's movements on his back. I wish I had some reins! Tom thought. Holding his hands over his eyes, Tom did his best to try and spot the plane. He knew that he could reach for and fire a flare in mere seconds, but if the plane was getting closer to him he wanted to wait. Seeing a flare in broad daylight from a few thousand feet in the air wasn't an easy thing to do and Tom knew it.

From the sound of the props, the plane was getting closer and closer to him. Tom still couldn't spot it and he thought the reason was the plane was directly in line with the sun from his position. So he grabbed the flare gun and fired. Half a minute later after he reloaded he fired again.

"Roger Hawaii. We are adjusting course," the pilot said and clicked off his mic.

"New orders?" the co-pilot of the C-130 asked his captain.

"They've found some debris up north. SAROPS has adjusted the search grid. We're way too south. Adjusting course."

"Roger that," the co-pilot said. When the captain turned the plane the co-pilot just missed what would have been the discovery of a lifetime – a few thousand feet below him a man riding on the back of a sperm whale had just released two flares. When the captain made his turn, the co-pilot stopped scanning the ocean.

If Tom had fired his flare even thirty seconds earlier the co-pilot would have surely seen it.

Chapter Twenty Eight

It was raining now. Not heavy rain; more mist, a drizzle. On this fourth day of his great sperm whale adventure, Tom's thoughts were on what might have been. When he fired the second flare he looked up in the sky and clearly saw the C-130. It could not have been more than five thousand feet above him. But the plane banked and turned due north the instant his flare exploded.

The only thing Tom could figure is that the aircraft had reached the end of its search pattern or had been ordered to start a new pattern. What were the odds of this happening the moment he fired his flare? Then again, what were the odds of Sydney being blown to bits or him being out here on the back of giant whale that he'd helped rescue twenty years before?

When he saw the plane, Tom's thoughts immediately shifted from the amazing experience he was living to his children back home in San Francisco. The search plane verified something he had assumed to be true, he was now officially listed as missing. Syd, Jonas and Jess must be in a state of panic. Oh how he wished that they could see him! It would have been the best of all possible worlds being spotted by the plane. They would have taken pictures of him riding on Henry and his kids could have watched them on TV!

But that was yesterday. Today the seas were up a bit, but not much. The swells weren't large enough to create whitecaps, but it was close. An hour or so after he started swimming, Henry stopped. When Tom heard the clicks he knew what was up, it was dinner time. On cue, Henry slipped under the surface and Tom was left alone.

"I wished you'd have picked a better day for this," Tom grumbled. He implemented his plan immediately. The first time he tried balance himself on his packs he fell over, but his second attempt was a success. The key to riding this way, just as Tom had assumed, was to keep his arms and legs outstretched, like outriggers on a canoe.

He lay there in the mist and gently rolling sea and opened a bottle of water. He took a small sip. His water supply was getting low, but if the last time Henry dove was any indicator soon fish would start popping up all around him. The liquid he consumed by eating the fish would be far more than a day's supply of water.

The sky was overcast, which was a blessing. Tom had to ration his aloe vera lotion and sunscreen. Because of the cloudy conditions he had chosen to forego any skin treatments today.

An hour passed, then two. Henry had not sent him any fish, but Tom wasn't worried. Perhaps today Henry will feed me when he's done eating, Tom thought. The seas calmed a bit and the rain let up. Tom fell asleep.

He woke up to the sound of a roar coming from the deep. Since he was not in the water he could not feel the pressure wave, but he knew what was happening. Henry was blasting fish for him again. How long have I been out of it? Tom asked himself. The sky was grey so getting an accurate position of the sun was impossible. He guessed he'd been asleep for two hours or maybe twice that long.

The fish began to pop up moments later. It wasn't flying fish this time, it was jack mackerel. Should I be in or out of the water now? Tom asked himself. In the water seemed the better bet because he could more easily maneuver his floating fish cleaning station around with his legs below the surface.

For whatever reason, Tom had no clue, the mackerel were dead, not stunned. And there were dozens of them coming up all around him. He grabbed one, severed its head and cleaned it and put in the side pocket of one of his packs. He didn't want to set the fish on top of the packs as he'd done previously – too many were lost using that strategy when Henry lifted him up out of the water.

He was on his seventh fish when he noticed something stir in the water a few feet away from him. He couldn't see anything so he assumed that one of the mackerel had survived and swam away to join what was left of the mackerel school.

Reaching out for fish number eight, Tom nearly lost his hand. A blue shark snatched the fish from him in a flash. Then two or three more blues began to feed on the mackerel. Dorsal fins began to pop up all around him. Tom was smack dabbed in the middle of a feeding frenzy.

Think Tom. Henry must be nearby. Would the whale be able to figure out that I'm in danger? Had Henry gone back down to the deep for a second helping of squid? Tom felt the rough skin of a blue shark brush up against his leg; it was like sandpaper being ground into his open wound. He screamed in agony. Tom knew that he had to get out of the water immediately.

He pulled himself up on the packs, but like the first time he tried it he fell over the other side. When he did, he was staring right into the eyes of a blue! The shark was as startled as he was and darted off. Tom made it when he tried to mount the packs the second time. But his butt was still in the water.

More sharks arrived and they were gorging themselves on the mackerel. Tom kept looking around, for some reason he thought counting the predators was important. He saw ten dorsal fins in the water, then twelve, then fifteen… then he stopped counting.

The blues were getting very aggressive. They were circling around his packs. Then one of the sharks tried to bite his left leg;

Tom avoided disaster at the last second when he jerked his foot back on the pack. When he did this he nearly toppled over, which he knew now was almost surely a death sentence.

He loaded both flare guns and put one in each hand. The next shark that opened its mouth and tried to munch on one of his appendages was going to get a red ball of fire sandwich. They were swimming all around him now, the mackerel were nearly gone. All that was left on the menu was human flesh.

Then Henry surfaced, but not directly under Tom. He was ten yards to Tom's port. The sharks didn't seem to notice the whale, or at least their behavior was unchanged. They were brushing up against the packs now, moving in for the kill.

Tom's eyes were on the whale. Henry moved abruptly in the water and while Tom could see his broad outline, he could not tell exactly what Henry was up to. Suddenly a large tail rose out of the ocean not five feet away from Tom. It tossed four sharks into the air and toppled Tom off of the packs.

The sharks were stunned and confused. Henry wasted no time. He hit a second group of the sea wolves and tossed a few more in the air. Now all the blues scattered; no doubt shocked that a sperm whale was flailing at them with its tail. Henry surfaced underneath Tom and assumed his logging position.

Looking to the side of Henry, Tom could see a couple of straggler blues darting back and forth no doubt completely befuddled. But after a few minutes the waters were clear of the predators. Tom had his packs properly positioned. Henry blew a short blast from his blowhole and they were off. There was still some time left before sunset and Henry was determined to keep moving, to stick with whatever plan he was executing.

Tom was shaking with fear. It wasn't until Henry had taken them well away from where he encountered the sharks did Tom's heart finally stop pounding through his chest.

◊   ◊   ◊

"Jonas, we need to talk," Gabriel said as he walked into Jonas' room. Jonas was busy playing a video game when his uncle interrupted him.

"Okay," Jonas said with trepidation. He had been expecting bad news.

"They found some of your father's clothing and a couple of other items floating in the ocean," Gabriel explained. "There is no sign of him or his sailboat."

"Dad's dead, isn't he. You can tell me, Uncle Gabe."

Gabriel grabbed Jonas' arms with purpose and looked into his nephew's eyes. "We don't know that, son. The Coast Guard says your father had a great life raft. After his boat sunk he probably climbed in the raft and now he's just waiting to be rescued. The experts think that most likely what's happened. Let's go with that for now."

"What am I gonna do... I mean without Dad. I was moving to Hawaii, ya know? I can't be stuck here with Mom and Harold. I just can't."

"Until they find my brother I'm staying here with you at your dad's place. That's a commitment, son. So let's take things one day at a time."

"Alright," Jonas said. "But Dad's out there all alone. Who is helping him? He needs help."

"Your father and I learned to sail together when we were kids. He ever tell you that?"

"I've heard a few stories," Jonas said.

"There was simply nobody better than your dad when it came to sailing. He won every contest we entered, finished first in almost every race. The man was born to be on the water. That's what he should have been doing for the past twenty years, but that's a whole other story.

"What I'm trying to tell you son is that while I can't sit here and promise you that your dad's okay because I just don't know, I do know that if there was ever anyone, and I mean anyone, who could get through something like this and live to tell about it its Thomas Campbell."

"I believe you, Uncle Gabe."

"Okay then. You and I gotta do something tonight."

"What's that?" Jonas asked.

"We gotta go see your mom. You need to tell her that you love her and that your dad's predicament is not her fault."

"I love mom ...but I'm not going to say it's not her fault, because it is."

"Really? How ya figure that, Jonas?"

"She divorced him and that's why he went sailing alone."

"You got it wrong son, on both counts."

"Uncle Gabe, you just don't -."

"Have I ever lied to ya? Even once in your whole life?" Gabriel asked.

"No, you never have."

"Then listen to me when I tell you this. Your Pop has wanted to sail solo in the tropics since we were boys. Your grandfather took us to Hawaii when Tom and I were teenagers and all your father could talk about was how he was going to sail to Hawaii all by himself when he got older. The only reason he didn't do it before now was because he loved your mom and you and Jess and devoted his life to being there for his family twenty four seven, three sixty five."

"But if Mom hadn't kicked him out -."

"Your parents still love each other. You get that, don't ya? Have you ever seen them talk nasty to each other or fight and fuss?"

"No," Jonas had to admit.

"Things happen in life. Being married is really tough, especially for people as smart and ambitious as your folks. You can love someone but not be happy living with them. I get it, that's an adult concept and a tough one to grasp, but you gotta know that both your dad and your mom tried as hard as they could to make it work. They both agreed to end the marriage; Syd didn't throw Tom out. She still loves your father very much. Believe that, son."

"But she -."

"But nothin', Jonas. Your mother needs your love and support. Your father, and I guarantee you this, would want you to step up and be a man here. He'd want you to do everything you could to help your mom through this. You know I'm telling you straight."

"Okay, I guess I need to think about this. Sorry," Jonas said.

"Hey kiddo. No need to say you're sorry. That's what uncles are for, to keep their nephews' heads screwed on straight. We'll take pizza with us over there; you won't have to eat any of that vegan crap."

"Thanks, Uncle Gabe."

"We're outta here in an hour. Take a shower and dress nice."

Chapter Twenty Nine

Two more days passed. Henry fed once more and Tom received another mackerel meal sans sharks. They were getting closer to the California coast now, perhaps only a few days away. Tom thought he had enough food and water to make it to land even if Henry didn't go fishing again.

But there was another problem. The third degree burn on Tom's leg was infected. There was a red ring around the charred flesh and it was expanding. A yellow discharge was oozing from the burn site and the lymph nodes in Tom's groin were blowing up like water balloons. If he got a blood infection or the wrong type of bacteria managed to... Why the hell didn't these emergency pack people include some penicillin in their first aid kits? He didn't want to think about the grim possibilities.

He was running a fever now and it was getting worse. Riding on the back of a sperm whale in the Pacific was a hot and messy thing to do. The smell was horrible and the wind whipping Tom took was abusive. But the fever... That could quickly become a serious problem. He had about a half a bottle of aspirin left, maybe fifty tablets. If he took four tablets every five hours, he might be able to control the symptoms enough to endure the final leg of his fantastic voyage.

Tom cut the remains of the second emergency blanket into a bandage that he wrapped around his leg. He secured the sides of the bandage with gauze tape. His main intent in doing this was to shield the burn from the sun and the spray and from whatever germs tried to invade the open wound. He knew that if Henry went for a dive again he would have to re-apply the entire bandage, so he left enough of the second emergency blanket uncut to make two more leg wraps.

Henry continued to move at a steady pace towards the southeast. Tom figured that no one would be looking for him in this area. However, he also knew that he would soon be entering waters that had a large amount of steady commercial ship traffic. He had six flares left to signal for help.

The first ship sighting he made was a glimpse of an oiler; since Tom had no binoculars or sunglasses observing objects on the water through the blinding sunlight was very difficult, especially in the late afternoon looking west. When he saw the ship he pulled out his flare gun, but he didn't fire. The freighter was headed northwest and Henry was moving southeast. He guessed that they were at least two miles apart and the gap was widening every second. Tom knew that the maximum distance an average person could see across the open water at sea level was around two and a half miles.

Near dusk, Tom spotted another vessel on the distant horizon. It was on a course that appeared would cross Henry's path. This was what he'd been waiting for! It seemed perfect. The vessel was large; it was a military ship or a freighter. As the minutes passed and the sun began to set Tom could see the ship more clearly. He guessed it was still two miles away or so, but if both Henry and ship continued to move in the same direction at the same speed they would pass very close to each other.

Then Henry stopped swimming and began his logging behavior. This shouldn't have surprised Tom in the least since the whale did this every evening at this same time.

"Henry, no!" Tom cried out. "Keep going! You've got to keep going!"

The whale did not react to Tom's outburst. From Henry's perspective, the day was over. He'd been motoring along at a steady clip for almost eleven hours and it was time to rest.

When Tom stopped shouting at Henry and looked up he noticed that the vessel, clearly a freighter, had made a course change. It was headed more north than west now, but it was still moving at the same speed.

Tom sent two flares into the twilight sky. He considered this to be an opportune moment to send up a flare because the sun had just set and whoever was on the freighter might be looking west just to admire the beauty. The flares would frame themselves nicely over the dull orange horizon.

"Carmen," the Chief Mate said. "I still got the... you know. Damn Chinese food! I told the cook something was wrong with it."

"You want me to relieve you, Butch?" Carmen joked. Carmen was a Deck Cadet, training to become an officer.

"Give me fifteen minutes. I'll be back by then… and in slightly better shape I hope," the Chief Mate answered.

"You got it," Carmen said.

The Mary Louise had just made the turn towards Long Beach harbor, still a day and half's pull away. The Chief Mate was on watch which meant he was in charge while the Captain was off duty, as was the case now. Going strictly by the book, a Deck Cadet could not relieve a Chief Mate, but all Butch had to do was visit the head.

Carmen wasn't worried. If anything happened of any significance he'd simply call Butch on the intercom and Butch would come running, even if his pants were at half-mast.

Bored more than anything else Deck Cadet Carmen grabbed the binoculars and looked to the east. They were still too far out to sea to spot land, but he wasn't looking for land he was looking for traffic. Out here the biggest navigational safety risk was colliding with a small craft that was in the wrong place at the wrong time.

Most of the time on Mary Louise there were two or three hands on deck doing one thing or the other, but when the sun set two seamen went below to fetch tools they needed to repair a sticky hatch and a third headed into a cargo bay to perform a routine check.

If Carmen would have looked behind him, he would have seen a couple of flares go up in the distance almost due west from Mary Louise. Anyone on the ship looking in that direction would have clearly seen the signal. The flares burned bright for sixty seconds and then went out.

"Why aren't you turning? Or sending up a response flare?" Tom said as he watched the ship move farther away. He reloaded his flare guns. He had four flares left. It was decision time. Should he use all four of his flares to try and signal the ship? Should he try one more? It was a judgment call to be sure, but making the wrong call could cost him his life.

For whatever reason, and it was more of a gut feeling than a well thought conclusion, Tom didn't fire another flare. As soon as the freighter disappeared he questioned his decision. Yes, I'm getting closer to shore every day, Tom reassured himself, but how long will Henry keep doing what he's been doing? And where was Henry's destination? A couple of miles off shore? An oil rig? Some kind of sperm whale rendezvous point?

Tom's leg was hurting worse now. The aspirin was not dulling the pain. If his leg didn't stop throbbing, Tom thought it might not be possible to sleep. Despite his desperate circumstances, a voice in Tom's brain was urging him not to let this experience end. You're riding a whale in the Pacific! Whether you live or die isn't as important as living this dream out to the fullest! When Tom had these thoughts they were often interrupted by images of his children. He knew that, regardless of any other concerns, he needed to do everything possible to get back to the world for them.

Tom didn't fire the flares at the ship because he wanted to stay with Henry; he thought there would be a better use for them later. As he lay down on Henry's back and tried to rest he hoped to God that he hadn't made a fatal mistake.

◊   ◊   ◊

"Okay, assessments," Commander Robinson ordered.

"If Campbell made into a life raft he could still be alive. We're well within the range of that possible outcome especially since we don't have a good estimated date on the sinking," Lieutenant Watkins said.

"Is that the consensus of your team?" Robinson asked.

"It is, sir," Watkins reported.

"What does SAROPS have to say?" Robinson needed to know.

"The projection is that the odds that Mr. Campbell is still breathing are less than ten percent," an NCO reported.

"Have we found any more debris?" the Commander asked.

"Negative. We've completed an intensive search of the area within forty square miles of where we found the clothes and the sail piece," Watkins said as she thumbed through her notes.

"Who is handling the media on this?" Robinson asked.

"Lt. Commander Ricks, sir. He's very experienced," Watkins answered.

"We absolutely do not release the SAROPS life expectancy projection to the family or to the media. We continue the search patterns for at least another seventy two hours. Send Ricks in here, please. Dismissed."

Chapter Thirty

It had been a day and a half since Tom saw the freighter. By his best estimate, he and Henry were within a hundred nautical miles of the California coast. They had to be unless he was completely wrong about either Henry's course or speed and that didn't seem possible.

This morning he didn't want to look at his leg. The stench told him everything he didn't want to know. The infection was getting worse, much worse. If the smell of his gammy leg overpowered the odor of the whale, then he was in real trouble.

But he undid the bandage anyway. He decided to use some of his precious fresh water to clean the wound. He also thought it couldn't hurt to crush a few of his aspirin tablets and gently sprinkle them on the burn. Not that it would do him any good at all if Henry got hungry and decided to dive for his lunch. Since the whale hadn't done this for four days now, Tom assumed Henry must be famished. Didn't sperm whales eat almost every day? Why would Henry not be eating?

Despite knowing the dangers of anthropomorphizing, Tom had come to believe that Henry was not regularly eating because the whale somehow knew that Tom needed to be brought back to shore as quickly as possible. Could this be true? Was the whale endangering his own survival to save a human being? Henry the selfless whale?

The skin in the burned area was totally black, which meant it was dead. Yellow pus was oozing out of the wound. The inside of Tom's right leg and his groin were swelled. He used the gauze bandages from the first aid to kit to clean it up as much as possible. Then he cut a new strip of emergency blanket and taped up his leg to hold the bandage in place.

He was dizzy too. Not a good sign. If he could not maintain equilibrium he was done for. The aspirins were not helping with the pain from his leg or from his ribs, which hurt like hell now too. His fever was in check at least enough for him to remain conscious.

"Henry, my friend," Tom said. Henry was still logging, he didn't seem to be in a rush to take off today. "We better hurry. I'll do my best, but I'm kinda running on fumes here. Do all -."

What was that? Tom asked himself. Just then Henry spouted and he was off. Tom was sure that he heard something. A minute or two later he heard it again. He didn't imagine it, it was a helicopter.

"San Diego Center, Echo Two Three Charlie," the pilot said into the mic.

"Echo Two Three Charlie," San Diego Center squawked back.

"Ah, San Diego Center be advised Echo Two Three Charlie... ah... stand by San Diego." The pilot stopped his transmission.

"Ricky, what the hell is that?" Gordon Helms asked his co-pilot, who was also his son-in-law.

"Looks like a signal flare. Wait one." Ricky Davis took out his binoculars and scanned the horizon. "It's a... I have no idea what that is!"

"Ah... Ricky. We're at the end of our range here. We're forty miles out to sea. Not a lot of time to be -."

"Okay Gordo. Remember now, I haven't had a drink in two years and I don't do drugs."

"Get to the point Ricky, was that a flare or wasn't it?"

"It was a flare. The guy who fired it is waving his arms at us."

"The guy?" Gordon said. "All I see is a whale down there, I think."

"The guy riding the whale is waving his arms at us. He fired the flare," Ricky explained.

"The guy... what?" Gordon grabbed his own binoculars and looked at Henry and Tom, who were now 200 feet below them and to their starboard.

"That's not possible... is it?" Gordon said.

"Is it more possible that we're both hallucinating?" Ricky asked.

Now both Gordon and Ricky were looking at Henry and Tom. The whale was continuing to move in the same direction at the same steady speed. Tom was busy waving his arms and shouting.

"Get out that fancy camera of yours, son," Gordon said. "I'm dropping down for a better look. There is no way I'm calling this in until you get pictures."

Ricky did as he was told. Gordon dropped to within fifty feet of Henry and Tom and Ricky clicked away. Tom was almost standing up now. Ricky leaned out of the chopper and waved at him.

"We gotta turn back," Gordon said. "We'll be landing on fumes as it is. Got the photos?"

"Yea, over twenty," Ricky said.

"This is incredible... I mean... what the hell just happened?"

"We saw a man riding on the back of a sperm whale and from the looks of the guy we better get help out to him right quick."

◈   ◈   ◈

"Yes, she's right here. I'll get her for you," Harold said. Sydney was still in the shower. Lately, she didn't get to sleep until almost dawn or get out of bed until the early afternoon.

"Syd!" Harold yelled. "The San Diego Coast Guard is trying to reach you. They say it's urgent."

All Sydney heard was "Coast Guard" and "urgent". She had been dreading this call. They had not found any evidence of Tom or his boat for days on end. The only possible outcome now seemed to be the inevitable, "We regret to inform you that..."

She rinsed her hair and got out of the shower. There was an extension in the bathroom. "This is Ms. Campbell," Sydney said as she picked up the phone and sat down on the toilet seat. She wasn't sure that she could remain standing after getting the news she expected to receive.

"Ms. Campbell, this is Commander Forest from the San Diego Coast Guard office. I'm calling about your ex-husband, Tom Campbell, who has been missing at sea for some days now."

"Yes..." Syd hesitated and said, "The San Diego Coast Guard? What do you have to do with this?"

"Are you sitting down Ms. Campbell?" Forest asked.

"As a matter of fact I am. Why? You can -."

"Thomas Campbell is alive. At least he was as of two hours ago. We are sending out a sea plane to pick him up right now."

"My God!" Sydney shouted. "Really! You know this for sure!"

"Yes ma'am. We have photos of him... Now here's where I need you to listen carefully to what I have to say. It's going to sound bizarre," Forest said.

"I can't believe it! I don't care how or why! My God, Tom is alive!"

"He's about thirty five miles off of the coast of Southern California. We have pictures of Mr. Campbell riding on the back of an adult sperm whale. The whale is bringing him back to land, or so it seems."

"What?" Sydney certainly wasn't expecting to be told that. "Say that again, and if this is your idea of a sick joke, so help me I will sue you for -."

"Thomas Campbell is on the back of an adult sperm whale. We have confirmed visual evidence of this. So does the world, there was nothing we could do to stop it."

"How is that possible?"

"We have no idea but... do you have access to the internet or television?" Forest asked.

Syd's *i Pad* was in the bathroom. She Googled CNN and there it was, the lead story - Thomas Campbell and his whale. She watched as the pictures rolled by. Tom looked like hell. He was burnt to a crisp and he had some sort of wound on his right leg. He was wearing a silver cape, but there was no doubt it was Tom.

Then it hit her. I couldn't be but...

"Commander Forest?"

"Still here, Ms. Campbell."

"Do you have a picture of the whale's tail?" Syd asked.

"Why on earth -."

"Yes or no, Commander?"

"Wait one," Forest said as he put Syd on hold. Harold had now joined Sydney in the bathroom.

"Harold, he's alive. Tom is alive!"

"That explains it then," Harold said.

"Explains what?" Syd asked.

"Why there are a dozen reporters on the lawn waiting for you to come out and make a statement," Harold explained.

"Ms. Campbell?" Forest said as he came back on the line.

"Yes, I'm here."

"We do in fact have a shot of the whale's tail. What is it that -."

"Is there a bite mark on the whale's fluke? Something that a shark would make if it took a hunk out of him?"

"Yes there is," Forest answered.

"I know that whale, Commander, and so does Tom."

Chapter Thirty One

Henry continued to swim at a steady pace in the same direction. Tom, on the other hand, was doing his best to dial it down and control his emotions. His mind was churning with various scenarios – even if the helicopter went down before it reached shore surely they called in the sighting. That had to be quite the radio transmission, Tom laughed to himself. "I'd like to report a man riding on a sperm whale. It looks like he might need some help."

He hoped that Syd and the kids had been told that he was alive. What an ordeal they've been through, Tom thought. He was also sure they were coming down to San Diego meet him.

It was all clear to Tom now. When he saw "Helms Flying School, San Diego California" printed on the chopper door everything clicked. Henry was taking him back to the beach where they'd first met two decades ago. It made perfect sense. From Henry's point of view that was Tom's home. Where else would he take him?

"I so wish I could talk with you," Tom said as he watched the ocean pass by at a gentle pace. "What you've done is… It may change things, Henry. My species has gotten a lot better about how we treat whales, but we need to do more.

"But ya know what? None of that really matters right now, does it my friend. You brought me home. That's stunning. I wish you could meet my kids. You'd love Jonas and he would absolutely go nuts over you. Jess, that's my girl, she might take a while to warm up to you, but -."

He wasn't sure how he missed it, but Tom had not heard the seaplane approach. Actually there were two seaplanes. They circled the whale a couple of times and then landed ten yards to Henry's port. The whale stopped swimming, as if he knew what was up.

"They've come to get me Henry," Tom said. "They want to take me the rest of the way home? What do you think?"

Henry spouted a large blast. Was he listening? Surely the whale had to know something important was happening.

A raft with two frogmen aboard motored over from one of the planes. They paddled in the final two hundred feet in an attempt, Tom assumed, not to startle the whale. At least five separate camera and video operators were filming the whole thing from the other plane.

"Hi there!" the frogman said. "I'm Ensign Harper and this is Chief Warrant Officer Palmer. You must be Thomas Campbell."

"Gentlemen you have no idea how happy I am to see you," Tom said.

"Who is your friend there?" Palmer asked.

"This is Henry. I'll bet were quite a sight."

"You might say that. Half the planet is waiting to watch the video those guys are shooting right now," Ensign Harper said, pointing back at the plane.

"Can you just slide right off?" Palmer asked. "I have no idea how you dismount from a sperm whale."

Tom took a deep breath. His leg was throbbing harder than ever before. His ribs felt like they were going to explode out of his chest. Every part of him was sore, burnt or bleeding. He had no business being in anywhere but in the ICU.

"How much father is it to San Diego?" Tom asked.

"You got about thirty miles to go, sir. Is that where… ah… Henry was taking you?" Palmer answered.

"Yep. Hey, you fellas got any medical supplies on those planes?" Tom asked.

"We brought along a doctor just for you, sir."

"He bring any meds along with him?"

"Yes sir," Palmer answered.

"Yea well… hey, this may sound strange but –."

Palmer and Harper started laughing. "No sir, nothing you could say right now would sound in the least bit strange."

"Give us a minute, will ya?" Tom asked.

"Take all the time you need," Palmer said.

Tom turned and faced Henry's huge head. He wanted to take in every wrinkle of his skin, every curve of his body, every sound and every smell. He loved this whale. The truth was he'd loved this whale for twenty years. To see him again and for Henry to do what he'd done for him was… it would take the rest of Tom's life to try and figure out just what it was.

"Old boy, what if I were to ask you to take me the rest of the way in? Do you want to finish what you started, or are you starving to death, my friend? I hate the thought of you going hungry on my account. I wish you could hear me, or understand what I'm trying to -."

Henry spouted through his blowhole and gently flapped his tail.

"Maybe you do understand… On a level I can't even imagine. Maybe you and your whale friends have always understood far more than we ever gave you credit for. Anyway, I'm with you big guy."

"Ensign Harper!" Tom shouted. "Would it be asking too much if I requested some supplies from you folks and an escort in rather than a plane ride home?"

"Are you serious, sir?" Harper asked.

"This whale has taken me a thousand miles on his back. I think he wants to finish the job. I know right where he's going, to Pacific Beach near where Balboa Road ends. He'll get as close as he can without beaching himself and then he'll let me off. You guys can pick me up there."

"How do you know that sir?" Palmer asked.

"Because twenty years ago he beached himself there and I found him. We got him back in the water and he remembered our kindness. He's paying back a debt to a friend. Who am I to stop him from doing that?"

"What do you need sir?" Harper asked.

"An IV drip of saline, another of morphine, treatment for severe burns and emergency surgery on my leg before I lose the damn thing. But for now I'll take ten bottles of water, whatever food you've got, a roast beef sandwich, I've been dreaming about those damn things, the strongest painkillers in the world and plenty of penicillin."

"Sir, my commanding officer is not going to like this at all," Ensign Harper said as he prepared to radio the plane with Tom's request.

"I'll be off the whale and on my way to the hospital in four hours or so. That's all it will take for Henry to cover thirty miles, Ensign. I'm afraid I have to insist," Tom said.

"Okay sir, but what if my CO orders me to remove you from the whale?"

"Look around, Harper," Tom said. Three news helicopters were now hovering around them and boats a plenty were headed their way. "I really don't think the Coast Guard wants to pull me off this whale. But, hey, let's be clear. If Henry changes his mind or gets spooked, I'm all yours."

Chapter Thirty Two

"I have no comment," Syd said as she and Gabriel, Jonah and Jess arrived at San Francisco International Airport to board a plane to San Diego. From the moment they stepped out of the cab they were mobbed by the media.

"Is this the same whale your ex-husband rescued twenty years ago?" a reporter shouted.

"Why was he out there all by himself?" another reporter barked.

"Is your divorce final? Does this change anything between you and Tom?" a third news hound yelled.

"That's enough," Gabriel said. Turning to Syd he whispered in her ear, "Airport security is headed our way. They'll take care of this pack of wolves."

Security quickly whisked them off to their gate. When they arrived other security personnel were posted to keep people at bay. Everyone wanted to know more about Tom and the amazing whale. It was the top news story worldwide. The latest wrinkle made a phenomenal story even more delicious.

"Oh my God," Gabriel said, looking at his smart phone. "Tom is riding the whale into shore. Look at this."

Gabriel handed Syd his phone. She watched in disbelief as a flotilla of ships and half a dozen helicopters surrounded Tom and the whale as Henry swam at his steady pace towards the shore.

"I have no explanation for any of this," Syd said. "But I'm so thankful he's alive."

"I have the coolest dad in the world," Jonas said.

Jessica didn't say a word, but her eyes were glued to her phone. She was absorbing everything the world was saying about her father.

◇　　　◇　　　◇

Tom felt good, really good. The Coast Guard boys brought him out a wash rag and soap. He gave himself a sponge bath perched on Henry's back. A toothbrush too! He never wanted to stop brushing his teeth and gums, it felt so good. They handed him a new swimsuit and wet suit top; gone was the silver cape and handmade head gear.

He spent almost fifteen minutes treating his leg wound with antibiotic ointments and burn creams. He properly bandaged it and then put a waterproof sleeve over the bandage. Ensign Harper gave him a pair of Oakley shades and a Coast Guard ball cap. He even got two roast beef sandwiches, both of which disappeared in less than a minute. Instead of water they gave him Gatorade to try and restore his electrolyte balance.

The pain meds and the penicillin were the real prizes. He took a couple hundred milligrams of Tylenol with codeine. He had five more of the little gems in a waterproof pill box in his wet suit pocket if he needed them.

Only one question remained. Would Henry go along with the program?

After Tom had finished preparing himself, the two seaplanes moved off. There were a dozen other small vessels around Henry now, but they were keeping a semi-respectable distance from the whale.

"Alright my friend, it's up to you. If you wanna take me home, let's go. Otherwise, you should go get something to eat."

Henry was waiting for this signal. "You are safe, you are safe" is what the whale heard. He spouted and the whale was moving again. There was just about four hours left before sunset. Tom knew exactly what time it was, 4:05 p.m., because the Coast Guard frogman had given him his dive watch to use for the trip.

"A little different than the first nine hundred and seventy miles huh, old boy," Tom yelled. "You're a media superstar now. Wanna go on *The Tonight Show* with me?"

For whatever reason, Henry picked up his pace a bit. Tom no longer had the emergency packs on Henry's back, but he did have a portable, waterproof ship to shore radio. The headset he was wearing was secured very tightly. If he fell off of the whale the headset would stay on. The life vest he had strapped on over his wetsuit top also gave him an added sense of security.

Tom could see land in the distance so he knew they were getting close. Boats pulled up next to Henry and people snapped photos and shot video. They shouted out things like, "We love you Henry!" and "Way to go Tom!" and "You're nearly there!"

An hour and a half into the final leg of his journey Tom heard a buzz in his headset. That meant he had a call so he tapped the earpiece.

"Hello," Tom said.

"Thank God you're alive," Sydney said.

"What do I look like on TV?"

"Like some kind of comic book superhero. 'Whale Man' maybe."

Tom laughed. "I'm sorry that I put you through this, Syd. I really am."

"I thought you might..." Syd started to cry. She didn't want to do that, but when Tom apologized like he'd done something wrong, she just lost it.

"Hey, I'm okay. How are the kids?" Tom asked.

"They're right here. They want to talk to you, but they have to wait their turn; me first."

"Okay. It's beyond wonderful to hear your voice."

"What happened out there?"

"Damn propane leak caused an explosion. The only thing I can figure is that the gas line was cracked. Propane must have pooled up in the bilge and when I went to light the oven…boom! The outfitters and I are going to have a word, believe that."

"So Sydney just blew up?"

"She just blew up. All that was left was me and a six by six foot piece of fiberglass. I nearly went down in the cabin. I thought I was dead and then Henry showed up. This trip has been one miracle after another."

"I called the Coast Guard in Hawaii. I made a real pest out of myself. Even got a Senator and a Congresswoman involved. I wanted to find you, I needed to find you."

"They just missed me."

"Who just missed you?"

"The search plane. It turned away at the last second, it just missed me."

"I love you, Tom."

"I love you too, Syd. How's Harold?"

"He's strong like you, in his own way. He's been my rock through all this."

"You should marry that guy."

"I plan to now that you're no longer a candidate for fish food."

"I want an invite to the wedding," Tom said.

"Seriously?"

"Yes, seriously," Tom confirmed.

"Jonas first. Here he is." Syd handed the phone to her son.

"Dad! I was so... I thought for sure you were dead," Jonas said.

"I guess I'm kinda like Jonah in the Bible. Remember that story?" Tom asked.

"You mean the whale swallowed you?" Jonas asked, astonished.

"No, but the whale did save me. He's dumping me out on the beach too, just like the whale did for Jonah," Tom said.

"I want to meet Henry," Jonas said.

"That's probably not possible, but all these people are taking a ton of pictures. We'll have plenty of memories."

"When you were missing… all I wanted to be was to be with you."

"So glad you weren't son. I nearly didn't make it. I want you to live a long and happy life."

"Mom says I have to give the phone to Jessica. Love you Dad! See you when you get to shore."

"Love you son."

"Daddy."

"Jess."

"If you ever do something as stupid as this again, I'll kill you," Jessica said.

"Yes ma'am."

"Something else."

"Okay," Tom said, smiling from ear to ear.

"I think you're the best dad in the whole world." With that Jess was gone. Tom heard rustling in the background and then, "I guess I'm the last guy on the phone train my brother," Gabriel said.

"Gabe! I thought you'd be there. Thanks for taking care of my family," Tom said.

"Freakin' trial got cancelled. A day too late. Sorry, man. I should have been out there with ya."

"Nah. You never were much of an animal guy. Henry is one huge, smelly beast."

"What's the story with that whale?" Gabriel asked.

"He saved my life, literally. I don't know how he found me or why he did what he did, but the only reason we're talking right now is because of Henry."

"I could kiss that whale."

"He'd probably like that, but no. I'll kiss you though. I can't tell you how much…" Now Tom was losing it.

"Hey, concentrate brother. I'm watching you on live TV. You've got ten miles to go."

"See you at the hospital?" Tom asked.

"I'll make sure you get a pretty nurse," Gabriel said.

Chapter Thirty Three

"I could walk in from here, Henry," Tom said as he looked around. They were less than a mile from the beach and rapidly approaching the shoreline. The water around Henry and Tom was filled with small vessels. There was literally no room between these watercraft; they were stacked three and four deep as if they were lining a parade route. Half a dozen helicopters were hovering above the beach. A blimp and several hot air balloons were jockeying for airspace just off shore.

All of the networks and cable news stations stopped broadcasting their regular programming and were carrying Henry and Tom's arrival live. Every whale expert on the planet and more than a few who were pretending to be were now the chief talking heads on the airwaves. Each of them had a theory as to why Henry was doing what he was doing.

On the extremes, one commentator said that he was sure that Henry was an alien intelligence from another galaxy and this was his way of saying hello; another argued that the whale was "following an elaborate stimulus and response scenario" that had been imprinted on him when he was rescued twenty years earlier and that to assume the existence of a higher, reasoning intelligence from "what we can observe and measure" was "pure folly".

"Now, don't go too far in, my friend. I don't think we could pull you off the sand a second time," Tom said.

"Mr. Campbell," a voice in his headset said.

"Roger that. I'm here," Tom answered.

"Uh, how far is Henry going to take you? Water depth at your current position is fifty feet and it's swallowing very quickly." A Coast Guard officer had been in constant communication with Tom since he and Henry took off on the final segment of their journey.

"I dunno. Should I ask him?" Tom joked.

"Sorry, lame question. Look behind you," the voice said.

Trailing a few yards behind Henry were two Coast Guard rescue rafts. The officer piloting the lead raft waved when Tom turned to look at him.

"Stay close. I think he's slowing down," Tom said.

Henry was indeed slowing, but he had not yet stopped. It appeared that Henry was determined to get as close to shore as possible before he dropped off Tom. Looking ahead, Tom saw that the beach was packed for as far as he could see with people and vehicles. Satellite TV trucks had driven on to the sand and giant boom lifts as well. A huge banner was hanging between two of the boom cranes which read, "Welcome Home Henry and Tom".

When Henry stopped, Tom took a deep breath. A loud cheer erupted from the throng on the beach. The noise grew in intensity, like the roar from the crowd at an NFL game.

The sun was setting in the west. As the daylight dimmed, camera flashes burst in from all directions. Tom had intended to remove his sunglasses after the sun went down, but now he decided against that. His eyes had been wind whipped and sun damaged on the open ocean for weeks, so he was not anxious to look directly at a bunch of flashing lights.

"Okay, Mr. Campbell. You're a hundred and fifty yards offshore and Henry is in thirty five feet of water," the Coast Guard Officer said over the radio.

"Roger that. Hey guys don't take this the wrong way, but I'm switching the mic off. I want a moment or two with Henry alone."

"Roger that. Are you going into the water sir?"

"Yes, right now. I'll give you the high sign when I'm ready for you to pick me up."

"Understood, sir. Standing by."

Tom slid off the whale and into the water. They were just beyond the surf line and the ocean was dead calm. For a few seconds, Tom took in Henry from this angle. Until now he had always been on top of the whale. Being by Henry's side gave Tom a different perspective; he felt smaller swimming by the side of the enormous creature.

Moving close to Henry's eye, Tom reached out and embraced his friend, as much as it was possible to embrace a fifty ton behemoth. When he did a million cameras all went off at once and another cheer rose from the boats floating nearby and the people on the shore. Henry clearly did not like the lights and the noise; he closed his eyes and flapped his tail a bit.

Tom raised his hand and showed his palm to the crowd, clearly asking them to stop shouting and cheering and to refrain from taking pictures. The television commentators caught on to Tom's signal and asked people to remain quiet and to turn off their cameras. After a minute or so, most of the onlookers complied with Tom's request. When the sound diminished and the lights stopped flashing, Henry opened up his eyes again.

"Henry, I know you can't understand my words. Maybe I shouldn't say that. We've had a lot of long talks, you and me. I've opened up to you more than I have to anyone else in my life. You don't speak English, but you do understand me on a level that goes beyond language. Somehow my intent, the heart of what I'm trying to say, gets through to you.

"I want to tell you how grateful I am, my friend. Before all this happened to me, I'd hear people say things like 'life is a precious gift' and 'live every day like it's you last'. I understood the meaning, but those words never resonated in me; I truly didn't get it. You've helped me to get it, my friend.

"Thank you for lifting me up on your back. Thank you for feeding me. Thank you for saving me from the sharks... but most of all, thank you for your friendship. You've given me something so precious, the chance to get to know you. You're a beautiful, kind, caring creature. All of those idiots who think whales don't have emotions or higher intelligence... just thinking about those fools now makes me want to laugh and cry at the same time.

"Hey, could we work something out? Like you meet me every Tuesday right here and take me for a ride for a couple of hours? I'd like to talk with you once a week! Pretty silly, huh. God I'll miss you!

"But you need to get the heck outta here. Go get something to eat. Take it easy and swim to Hawaii, if that's where you were going. Live a long and happy whale life. More than anything else I'd like to see you again, but I know that'll probably never happen."

Tom raised his hand and motioned for the Coast Guard raft to move in and pick him up.

"Goodbye my friend. May you always be healthy, happy and free. I love you, Henry."

Henry heard something new in the land creature's voice. He heard the tone of "I am one with you, I am one with you", a tone that Henry had only heard before from his close whale relatives. So Henry clicked back, "I am one with you, I am one with you."

Until Tom was safely in the rescue raft, Henry didn't move. Once he saw that the land creature he trusted was inside the object that floated on the water he clicked "I am one with you" one last time and slowly swam away.

"Okay, fellas," Tom said to his Coast Guard handlers, "it's time that I got some value out of my expensive medical insurance."

Chapter Thirty Four

Henry was famished. He had eaten less than half the food he needed to over the past ten days. After he was sure that the land creatures on the floating objects had helped the land creature he trusted, he swam away and went down deep to feed.

Although he did not normally feed here this time of year, Henry knew these waters well. There was still squid and fish to be had in the usual places and after a couple of hours of eating Henry was full.

He sent out codas searching for other sperm whales in the area, but he didn't get an immediate response. For the past year or so Henry had been swimming with two other young bulls. At twenty years old it was almost time for Henry to think about mating, but that biological alarm clock had not yet rang.

For the next few cycles of light and darkness Henry planned to remain in the area and feed. Once he built his strength back up he would swim west to the middle of the ocean where small areas of land stuck up through the waves. This time of year the food was abundant near these small areas of land. He was confident that his bull whale cousins were already there and feeding.

Henry rose to the surface and began logging. When he did he experienced the sensation that something was wrong, something was missing. This feeling disturbed Henry so much that he swam for a bit and then began logging again. The feeling of incompleteness returned. It was unpleasant and Henry did not know what was missing or what he should do next, but then he recalled that for the first time in many light and dark cycles the land creature he trusted was not riding on his back. That's what was missing...

When he found the land creature he trusted in the middle of the water and put him on his back, Henry knew that he had to move, and not move, in certain ways in order to help the land creature survive. Land creatures did not survive long in the water if they are not on top of the objects that float. All sperm whales knew that, but Henry had no base of knowledge passed down to him by other whales that taught him what to do to help a land creature that was floating alone in the water far from land.

Henry learned what to do by paying attention to the land creature's sounds. The land creature he trusted did not click, so Henry could not understand what his sounds meant, but he could understand from the tone of the sounds whether or not the land creature was happy and safe, or worried and full of fear.

Long ago, so far back that Henry had to think hard to recall a memory that was now incomplete, the land creature he trusted helped him get safe. Henry, like all sperm whales, always helped his fellow whales. He was born and bred with an ethos – take care of all whales and they will take care of you. Work together for survival. If a whale is sick or injured, make sure that they are fed and protected until they are no longer sick or injured, until they are safe.

When Henry saw the land creature he trusted floating on top of the small object in the middle of the water, he knew that the land creature was in distress. He transferred his instinctual and learned predisposition to help other whales on to the land creature he trusted.

But now the land creature he trusted was gone. Henry had done what he was supposed to do, he helped an injured whale as best as he could. Henry knew that the land creature he trusted was not another whale, but he believed that he deserved to be cared for like another whale.

This was not as much of a conscious choice for Henry as it was a response to the circumstances put in front of him. The land creature he trusted, the land creature he had relied on when he was stuck on the sand, the land creature who comforted him in the dark time after his mother was killed, this land creature deserved to be treated like a sperm whale.

Understanding why he felt incomplete kept Henry from worrying that something else was wrong, but it did not lessen his desire to be complete. Despite having to survive on less food while he carried him, Henry liked taking the land creature he trusted back to the place on the sand where the land creature lived. Helping the land creature he trusted reminded Henry of his days as a calf and how his mother had fed and protected him. Doing the same for the land creature he trusted made Henry feel like he was doing for the land creature what his mother had done for him.

Many sperm whales did not consider the small creatures that lived on the land to be of any value. Codas had been passed down through generations of sperm whales warning that these small land creatures were very dangerous and that they killed sperm whales. Neither Henry nor his mother had ever seen a small land creature use one of the floating objects to hurt whales, expect for when Henry's mother was killed.

But Henry's experience with small land creatures had taught him a different lesson - land creatures had value. They were worthy of life. They were not predators like the big fish with the sharp teeth or the creatures that made sounds like sperm whales but acted like big fish with sharp teeth.

As Henry was at ease in the moonlight enjoying the pleasant sensation of a full belly, he had the thought that he missed the sounds the land creature he trusted made. At night the land creature would make sounds for long periods. Henry learned to listen to these sounds and to enjoy hearing them. They were not as beautiful to his ears as were the codas of his fellow whales, but they were pleasant in their own way.

Henry wanted to see the land creature he trusted again. He did not know when or where this meeting might occur, or whether it would be a few light or dark cycles away or much longer.

When Henry returned to his bull male cousins he would tell them about the land creature he trusted and the journey they had taken together. Henry knew that they would probably not understand, but they would listen and believe him because sperm whales always listened to and believed what other sperm whales had to say.

Chapter Thirty Five

"How long has he been in there?" Sydney asked.

"Going on four hours now," Gabriel answered. "Coffee?"

"Any more coffee and I'll be bouncing off the walls. How are the kids?" Syd wanted to know.

Gabriel Campbell walked from the general surgery waiting area of the UCSD Medical Center down the hall to another lounge that had vending machines and televisions. Jonas and Jessica were busy talking with a small group of kids, no doubt fielding questions about their suddenly world famous father. Gabriel left them alone and returned to his sister-in-law's side.

"They're just fine, hanging out with some new pals. Have you talked with Harold in the last couple of hours?" Gabriel asked as he sat down in the same chair where he'd been parked since six a.m.

"He's in Portland. I asked him to come down and be with us, but he thought it was way too awkward. He's right, I guess. I love him, Gabe. Harold and I are good for each other."

"I know. Things in that department should get a little easier in the -."

Gabriel quit talking because a team of doctors emerged from the surgery suites. The lead surgeon on the team, Dr. Kamin, spoke first. "Tom is out of danger. I guess he was never really in danger, but his leg sure was. I have to tell you when I looked at that leg… Let's just say I was skeptical. I can only imagine the types of bacteria that the wound was exposed to… Anyway, his infection is under control and his leg, while I'm not yet willing to give you a completely green light yet, right now I'm confident that his leg does not need to be amputated. He's a lucky man. Even an hour or two more of exposure and, well… there is no sense speculating further."

"What about his ribs?" Gabriel asked.

"Severely bruised, none broke. All of his other burns were treated too. A couple were second degree, but the only infected burn was on his leg. His general health has also suffered, he's lost a lot of weight, but he'll recover," Kamin explained.

"How soon can we see him?" Syd asked.

"Let him wake up and eat, get his bearings. Later on today, this afternoon I suppose. As soon as he wakes up and we see that he's not in distress, we'll wheel him up to his room."

"Thanks, Doctor. Thank you so much," Sydney said.

"You're coming with me, right?" Dr. Kamin said.

"With you where?" Syd asked.

"To the conference room. They're all set up. In ten minutes, I'm holding a medical news conference."

"No, not me. Gabriel?" Syd asked.

"Okay, sure. Why not," Gabriel said. "I might as well volunteer."

"Thanks," Kamin said. "It would be better if a family member were present. I just have to say that…"

"Have to say what, Doctor?" Syd said.

"Tom is an extraordinary man… I wouldn't have made it half as long. And that whale thing… it's unreal."

"Ready, Doc?" Gabriel intervened because he knew that Syd did not like talking about Tom with strangers.

"Let's go," Kamin said.

◊   ◊   ◊

"Hi Dad," Jonas said as he walked in his father's hospital room.

"Come over here, but stay away from the leg," Tom said. Tom's right leg was suspended in a sling a foot off the bed.

After they had hugged for a minute, Jessica took her turn with her father.

"You're just about the most famous person in the whole world, Daddy," Jessica said. "It's amazing."

"Yes you are, honey," Tom said, smiling at his little girl.

Before the kids were allowed in, Sydney and Gabriel spent half an hour alone with Tom. They were sitting off to the side of his bed now.

"You're gonna be super rich, huh," Jonas said.

"Why do you think that?" Tom asked.

"Kids were offering me fifty bucks if I could get them your autograph, that's why," Jonas bragged.

"Yea, me too, Daddy. A couple of girls gave me these pictures and said if you'd sign them they would give me a hundred dollars," Jessica added.

"Ah well, every blessing comes with its own set of curses," Tom moaned.

Sydney laughed and said, "At least you know who to go to for the book deal."

"Yea, like we talked about Harold can take care of all that. Okay kids, gotta cut it short. We're going to have dinner in here just the five of us, but I promised to talk to some reporters first. If I give them forty five minutes, they will leave me alone for a couple of days. Sound like a good deal?" Tom asked.

"Yea, were outta here," Gabriel said. "They've got an empty room down the hall where we can hang out while you do your thing."

After his family left four reporters, who had been selected by a random drawing, were allowed into Tom's hospital room. They knew that from the moment they walked in the clock was ticking, so they didn't waste any time.

"Mack Reynolds, LA Times. Tom, what happened out there? Your boat exploded? That's what we were told by the Coast Guard, just want to confirm that."

"The propane gas lines onboard were leaking, or at least one of them was leaking. When I lit my oven, propane in the bilge exploded and turned Sydney into splinters in an instant."

"Shirley Downs, MSNBC. How long were you on the raft, the piece of fiberglass?" The reporters had been given a briefing sheet from the Coast Guard which related the basic facts about what happened to Tom.

"My best guess is three weeks, give or take a day or two either way."

"John Kirkwood, CBS News. Tell us what it was like when the whale rescued you."

Tom took a deep breath and said, "I was sure that I was dying. When I slipped into the water, I had basically given up all hope of survival. I had no food or water and I had not drank or eaten a thing for several days. Rather than slide into oblivion, Henry lifted me out of the water and took me to where the two emergency packs were floating."

"The whale took you where?" Kirkwood followed up.

"Some distance away, half a mile or more I'd guess. Two of Sydney's emergency packs were floating there. Henry took me to get 'em. They had enough water and food in them to revive and sustain me for a while."

"What did the whale -."

"Excuse me. John is it?" Tom asked.

"John Kirkwood, yes."

"John, my friend has a name. It's Henry. Yes, he's a sperm whale but he's also my friend. Please call him by his name. I'd appreciate it."

"Amy Dinkler, New Yorker Magazine. "Tom, why did you name your friend Henry?"

"Next question," Tom said.

"Excuse me. You insist that we call him Henry. Why is asking you why you named him Henry off limits?" Amy asked, clearly annoyed.

"Because it is. Next question, and it better not be about why I named him Henry or this interview is over," Tom answered tersely.

"There is some reference made in the Coast Guard report to Henry feeding you," Mack Reynolds picked up, clearly interested in diverting attention away from the sensitive topic. "Exactly how did he do that?"

And so it went for exactly forty more minutes when Tom said, "Time's up" and the reporters left. None of them dared asked anything more about why Tom named the whale Henry, although the answer to that question now became the one everyone in the world most wanted to know.

Chapter Thirty Six

"Aren't you getting tired of telling the story?" James Banks asked. "I mean it's the greatest story ever told in cetacean research, but still... I'd completely understand if you'd like a break from the endless chain of speeches and events."

"How much money are we talking about?" Tom asked.

"They think they can raise over $50,000 at the event in Portland. Your speaking fees alone are $35,000. Add that $85,000 to the $720,000 you've brought in so far this quarter from your personal appearances and we are well on our way to the $1.25 million we need to start building the new center," Banks answered.

"I'll go. I have to check with Jonas though. He may want to come with me; might be a good chance to sneak some time in with his mom."

"Good enough. I promise you after the second quarter of the year the speaking circuit is over. You've done your duty and then some, Tom."

"Well, I hope you hired me for more than just my whale stories. I'd like to think that -."

"We did. We're damn lucky to have you on staff. Even at half time you're a boon to this Institute. You know, once you finish your Ph.D. program in a couple of years you can have your pick of jobs anywhere on the planet."

"I like it here, Jim. Not goin' anywhere... Hey, I forgot to tell you. The book comes out in six months. I proofed the final manuscript yesterday. *Henry and Tom* – catchy name, don't you think?"

"You gave the whale top billing. Such humility," James joked.

"Well, what can I say? He's made all my dreams come true. Did my agent -."

"Yes, we got a check for $200,000. Add that to your total too. There was no need to give us ten percent of your book advance, Tom. Twenty percent of the royalties was far too generous to begin with."

"The money is for Henry. We're going to build a cetacean research facility here that is second to none. His name goes on the building too, don't forget that."

"Does Henry have a last name? Seems only proper."

"He's a whale, Jim. Whales don't have last names, everybody knows that."

"Alright traveling man," Jim said, laughing. "I'll get out of your hair. You're gone for ten days this time, right? The gigs in Japan?"

"Back before you know it," Tom said.

"Be sure to check in once in a while. As silly as it is, technically you're an employee here; an employee who pays almost a quarter of everyone's salary these days, but still an employee."

James shut the door behind him. Tom spent a few minutes organizing his desk and loading the files onto his *i Pad* that he would need in Japan. He had not been to Asia yet; there simply had not been time. He was looking forward to seeing Tokyo and touring the country's finest marine research facilities.

Tom's office overlooked Kane'ohe Bay and looked back towards the island of Oahu. It was a million dollar view and then some. Across the bay and up on the mountain was Tom's new house. It was understated given his dramatically increased net worth, but

Tom was beyond happy with his three bedroom home. He loved the fact that he could look out his office window and see where he lived.

Starting next month Tom would be both the Director of Fundraising and Public Relations for the Hawaii Institute of Marine Biology (HIMB) and a doctoral student in marine biology at the University of Hawaii. Add to that bestselling author and in demand public speaker and his life was very full.

It had been almost eight months since Tom's experience with Henry. Most nights, when he was home, he spent hanging out with Jonas who was thriving at his new private high school. His son's grades had vastly improved along with his general attitude. Almost every day after school Jonas went sailing or diving, the two new passions in his life. Jessica visited her father every few weeks, but she was happier living with Syd and Harold in California, who were now husband and wife.

The last thing Tom wanted to be was a celebrity, but he chose to use his fame to help create a new world class research facility at HIMB that would study all aspects of marine mammal biology. When he got his doctorate, he was promised a faculty position from which, in twenty years or so, he planned to retire.

On Tom's desk were pictures of his children, Gabriel and his family and his father and mother. On the wall behind his desk was another photo, blown up to portrait size and framed.

In the picture was an older man, he looked to be over sixty and weathered, and a young boy, maybe twelve or thirteen. They were standing on a pier by a skiff which was tied to cleat on the dock. In handwriting on the bottom corner of the picture was written, "Love ya, kid. Grandpa."

"Keep an eye on the place while I'm gone, Grandpa Henry," Tom said as he switched off his office lights and left.

Henry was the man who taught Tom how to sail. His father was too busy earning a living to spend every afternoon on the water with his son, but Henry Campbell was a retired Naval Officer who had nothing but time on his hands. He loved to be with both of his grandsons, but especially with Tom because Tom was the one who most shared his passion not only for sailing, but for the sea and everything about it.

Tom was sixteen when Grandpa Henry died of a stroke. Young Tom Campbell was devastated and not only because he'd lost a dear and sweet grandfather, but because he'd lost his best friend. Whatever Tom needed, Henry provided. He gave love and attention in abundance – these things and so much more flowed freely from Henry to Tom Campbell.

The day when Tom met the juvenile sperm whale stranded on the beach he had been thinking about his grandfather. He was thinking mostly that he would have loved for his grandpa to have met Syd and how thrilled Henry would be that his grandson was working at a prestigious marine center like Scripps.

Right from the start there was something about the whale that reminded Tom of his grandfather, but he wasn't sure exactly what it was. Perhaps more than anything else it was the connection, the bond that formed between Tom and the whale. While that bond developed rapidly, it was as meaningful and lasting as the tie between Tom and his grandfather.

The whale's name was Henry. No other name fit or made any sense at all.

Authors' Biographies

Author Michael Atkins

Michael Atkins has been exploring the world's oceans as a sailor, scuba and deep submersible diver, marine biologist, oceanographer, and conservationist since 1986. He received his PhD in biological oceanography from MIT and has logged over 200K miles at sea. He considers sustainable stewardship of marine ecosystems to be his life long calling and passion.

Author Wid Bastian

Wid Bastian is a novelist and screenwriter. His screen- play work includes the upcoming feature film, Themi, scheduled for release in 2016. As a ghostwriter, Wid has penned numerous novels and memoirs that have been published both in America and abroad. An avid scuba diver since the late 1980s, Wid loves the ocean in general and whales in particular. When he's not working in Los Angeles, Wid enjoys being home in Logan, Utah with his fiancee Elaine, her two kids, four cats, a dog and other assorted critters.

Social Media

www.henryandtom.com
www.facebook.com/henryandtom
www.twitter.com/henryandtom

Made in the USA
San Bernardino, CA
21 May 2015